**"It may shock you, Eloise, but your misery is not actually my goal. What I want is my child."**

"Why?"

"Is it not the most natural thing in the world to want your child?"

She stared at him. "You and I both know that it is not."

"Eloise..."

"No. I know that I don't have a lot of power here, but I have had so little choice in my life, Vincenzo. Surely you must want more than to hide me away in this place. Surely I deserve more than that."

"What is it you want?" he asked.

It came to her in a moment, because the truth was, it would be...a wonderful thing for her child to know its father.

It was only her fears of that palace, of that life, that truly held her back.

"Make me a beautiful Christmas there at the palace. Show me that there's something there other than what I remember. Other than that dreadful...awful empty feeling that I always get in the palace. Show me that there can be more."

## Pregnant Princesses

*When passionate nights lead to unexpected heirs!*

Vincenzo, Rafael, Zeus and Jahangir are princes
bound for life by their ruthless quests to rebel
against their tyrannical fathers. But their plans will
be outrageously upended when forbidden nights
with forbidden princesses leave them facing the
most shocking of consequences...and convenient
marriages that spark much more than scandal!

Read Vincenzo and Eloise's story in
*Crowned for His Christmas Baby* by Maisey Yates

Available now!

Read Rafael and Amalia's story in
*Pregnant by the Wrong Prince*
by Jackie Ashenden

Read Zeus and Nina's story in
*The Scandal That Made Her His Queen*
by Caitlin Crews

And look out for Jag and Rita's story
by Marcella Bell

Coming soon!

# *Maisey Yates*

——

# CROWNED FOR HIS
# CHRISTMAS BABY

HARLEQUIN
PRESENTS

Recycling programs for this product may not exist in your area.

ISBN-13: 978-1-335-56818-2

Crowned for His Christmas Baby

Copyright © 2021 by Maisey Yates

This edition published by arrangement with Harlequin Books S.A.

For questions and comments about the quality of this book, please contact us at CustomerService@Harlequin.com.

Harlequin Enterprises ULC
22 Adelaide St. West, 40th Floor
Toronto, Ontario M5H 4E3, Canada
www.Harlequin.com

Printed in U.S.A.

**Maisey Yates** is a *New York Times* bestselling author of over one hundred romance novels. Whether she's writing strong, hardworking cowboys, dissolute princes or multigenerational family stories, she loves getting lost in fictional worlds. An avid knitter with a dangerous yarn addiction and an aversion to housework, Maisey lives with her husband and three kids in rural Oregon. Check out her website, maiseyyates.com.

### Books by Maisey Yates

### Harlequin Presents

*Crowned for My Royal Baby*

### Once Upon a Seduction...

*The Prince's Captive Virgin*
*The Prince's Stolen Virgin*
*The Italian's Pregnant Prisoner*
*The Queen's Baby Scandal*
*Crowning His Convenient Princess*

### The Heirs of Liri

*His Majesty's Forbidden Temptation*
*A Bride for the Lost King*

Visit the Author Profile page
at Harlequin.com for more titles.

To Megan, Jackie and Marcella—what's better than alpha heroes? Alpha heroes that you get to write with your friends.

# PROLOGUE

THEY WERE THE most notorious, shocking, dissolute group of rakes to ever grace the hallowed halls of Oxford. And given the school's illustrious and rather lengthy history, that was truly saying something.

Of course neither Prince Vincenzo Moretti, heir to the throne of Arista, nor his friends, Sheikh Jahangir Hassan Umar Al Hayat, Prince Zeus and Rafael Navarro, bastard child of a king of Santa Castelia, would ever say it themselves.

There was no need.

Their reputations preceded them.

With great pomp and circumstance. From the mouths of men who envied them, wishing only to find themselves ensconced in the afterglow of their power, as if it might give them even the tiniest bit of access to the women that they enjoyed, or the excess that they acquired with the snap of a finger.

And of course, from the women.

The women who declared themselves ruined for all other men, who sighed wistfully about the pleasure they had experienced at their royal hands and would never experience again.

For surely, no man alive could match the prowess of these ruthless royals.

And they could not. Vincenzo himself had no qualms about basking in the benefits of such a reputation.

Of course, his father believed that he would put on the public face required of him for all the world to see. All the while, seeking his own pleasure and lining his own pockets, as their people lived in spartan circumstances.

Vincenzo had begun to combat that with the establishment of many charities, using covert networks he had created outside of his country to bring money in that his father could not touch. Money that appeared to be foreign aid that he would keep his hands off in the name of keeping relations strong between other nations.

But that was not Vincenzo's only plan. No. He was playing a long game. He could not move, not now. His mother's health—mentally and physically—was fragile. Especially after the scandal three years ago that had rocked Arista. After...

Eloise.

He refused to dwell on her.

He would not.

The destruction of the monarchy would end his mother. And he could not bear that. He would protect his mother. No matter what.

His mother had loved the palace once—and Arista. And the one thing she enjoyed still in life was her role as Queen. He could not let her see what he would do to the royal family. The royal line.

For he would not produce an heir. Never. He refused. He would not carry on the royal line of Arista. He would allow his country to change hands. To go into the hands of the people. And he would make sure that his father knew this before his death. This legacy… It was the only thing his father cared for.

And Vincenzo would see it destroyed.

Yes, his reputation as a notorious, shocking, dissolute rake was truly one that would make even the hardest of harlots clutch their pearls. But if they knew what he really was, if they knew what he truly intended to do… They would expire from the shock.

"A toast," he said, looking around the room that served as their clubhouse, where they conducted their meetings—all of them already earning their own money hand over fist, carving their own place in the world apart from the legacies of their dubious fathers. "To being unexpected."

"It could be argued," Rafael said, "that your rebellion might be seen as deeply expected."

"It will never be expected by our fathers. Who are far too prideful to think that anyone could surprise them in the least. But I have no trouble playing a long game."

"No indeed," Zeus said, looking down into his

glass of scotch. "But I think, my friend, that you will find I am not a patient man. I prefer the game short. Hard and brutal."

"I'm all for brutality. But I find brutality is much more effective when meted out strategically."

"I didn't say I wasn't strategic," Zeus said, grinning broadly. "I said I wasn't patient." He lifted a shoulder. "Brutality now. Brutality later. Brutality all around." He waved a laconic hand and settled more deeply into his resolute lounging position.

"I admire your thinking," Jag said, one leg thrown out in front of him, his arm slung over the back of the couch. He elevated casual disdain to high art.

"For my part, I intend to let my father's kingdom…" Vincenzo swirled the glass and watched the amber liquid spin, an aromatic tornado. He lifted the scotch to his lips. "I will not produce an heir. Ever."

"How nice for me that it is not expected," Rafael said. "As a bastard, it is my younger legitimate brother who will inherit control of the kingdom, and the concern of carrying on the line is his. Not mine."

"My father cares so greatly for the reputation of our country," Jag said. "My greatest delight would be to find a woman he would see as desperately unsuitable."

"Only *one* woman?" Zeus asked. "I myself intend to acquire an entire stable of them. But no heir. Never that."

"A toast to that," Vincenzo amended. "To unsuitable women, revenge served hot or cold and to never falling in line."

# CHAPTER ONE

ELOISE ST. GEORGE did not feel merry or bright. The snow falling outside felt like an assault, as did the roaring fire, beautiful evergreen garland and cheery Christmas tunes. Yet she was responsible for it all— save the snow. A resolute rebellion against the depression that was threatening to swallow her whole.

Christmas Eve.

She was without a Christmas tree. Since it was still back in Arista. With him.

She had hung garlands, wreaths and other hallmarks of cheer. She had baked cookies and decorated them, had made herself a beautiful dinner. But she wasn't feeling… Any of it.

She had made Christmas a happy time for herself all these years, in defiance of her upbringing. She'd always been happy to celebrate it alone, in her historic stone house in Virginia, which could not be more picturesque.

But alone felt… Alone this year. Truly, deeply.

With all the snow piled outside, she'd managed

to get Skerret, her foundling cat, to finally come inside from the cold.

The little gray creature was curled up by the red brick fireplace in a contented ball, purring.

It should be wonderful.

It wasn't.

She put her hand down on her rounded stomach.

It would have been wonderful. If not for Vincenzo Moretti.

And the fact she was currently carrying the heir he had vowed to never create.

*Seven months earlier...*

This was the address he had been given, but Prince Vincenzo Moretti could not reconcile the crumbling manor before him with the woman he knew Eloise St. George to be. He remembered her vividly.

She had lived at the palace from the time she was six years old, and he had found her disruptive. He was four years her senior and at ten he had been deeply serious. He had also suspected that her presence was emblematic of something that was wrong in the palace. He had been correct.

Her mother had come to the palace to be his father's mistress. He didn't advertise that, of course. Not the Upright and Honorable King Giovanni Moretti. He gave her an official job title to conceal her real purpose. But even at ten, Vincenzo knew.

He could see it in the decline in his mother's health.

He had resented Eloise at first. Had seen her as the mascot of his father's perfidy and her mother's sins.

But reluctantly, slowly, over the years she had become his… Friend.

A shock for an arrogant princeling who had never befriended anyone in his life.

Then he'd gone off to university and met Rafael, Zeus and Jag. And when he'd returned home…

Eloise had been a woman. And things had taken a turn.

He'd found her beautiful. Captivating. She'd seemed fragile and still so innocent. But when she'd… When she had told him she wanted him, he'd turned her away. Out of deference to her youth, her innocence.

Because she had not chosen life in the palace. Had not chosen a life where she was forced to know him and he'd felt that she should… Go and experience life and men she had chosen.

But her true colors had been revealed after. Not innocent. Not his friend.

Not…

It did not matter except in the way she might be useful to him now.

The way that she might enhance his plan.

His father had been involved in one scandal. Only ever one.

Eloise.

She had become the symbol of an old man's folly. A man who could never have resisted the wiles of an eighteen-year-old beauty hell-bent on seduction.

His father's only sin.

While publicly, Vincenzo committed many.

For all the world to see, Vincenzo was a disappointment. A man who glutted himself on every indulgence available, a man who engaged openly in the kinds of behavior his father engaged in privately.

But in secret, it was Vincenzo who was saving Arista, and they would never know it until after his father died.

But he would not save it in the manner his old man wished. For he would not produce an heir. He would let the monarchy burn.

And he would be all the gladder for it.

His father was an old man now. And it was time to begin dismantling his legacy. His facade. For he wished to do it where his father could still see. Exposing his financial malfeasance and his mistreatment of his wife. The beloved Queen of Arista.

His poor mother had been... Disgraced in the end.

His father had told the country she'd fallen into a depression and had blamed a weak spirit.

Not his own actions of course.

His father had damaged his mother's legacy, and Vincenzo would *destroy* the King's.

And it began here. Though he had not expected

this ramshackle collection of stones with ivy climbing up the side of it. Nor had he expected the crooked wrought iron gate with honeysuckle wound through the spires.

Eloise St. George he would've expected to live in an ultramodern flat paid for by her latest conquest. Somewhere near clubs and shopping and all the other vices her kind enjoyed. But not this. This place out in the middle of nowhere. Clearly, he had seen that it was near nothing when he had looked it up on the map, but he had expected something grander.

Or that perhaps she had built her own row of shops that had not yet appeared in the mapping program. For he could hardly imagine the girl that he'd known moldering away in the countryside. Least of all in a place like this.

He pushed open the gate, which creaked and caught on a vine that grew out of the cobbled walk.

It was a hazard, this place. He slammed the gate shut, though it did not close all the way, and he strode up the walk, careful not to catch his foot on any of the uneven stones. Nature, it seemed, had taken over this place. There were hedges, large trees wrapped in creeping vines. Most of the garden was shaded, with sun, golden as it was in mid-May, breaking through each time the breeze twisted the leaves.

It was hot. Far too hot for the bespoke suit that he was wearing, but it was not in his nature to yield to the elements. He preferred to force them to bend to him.

Why she had chosen to make her escape here in this rather rural corner of the United States he did not know. It made no earthly sense to him. Which in and of itself was a mystery, because Eloise should be simple. Her mother certainly had been. And as far as he'd been able to tell, Eloise was the same.

Her mother, protected by her title of Personal Assistant had spent lavishly and lorded her position over the household staff.

And Eloise, he had been certain, was driven by much the same things. He might have believed she was different once.

But he'd learned.

Yes. Eloise was no different than her mother. Which was why he was confident that he could enlist her services. Either through blackmail or bribery. It did not matter to him which.

He stood at the front door, blue with a cheerful wreath hung at the center. He could not imagine Eloise taking the time to hang a wreath at the center of her door.

She must have staff to see to such things.

Perhaps that was the piece he was missing.

Perhaps this was where her protector had installed her. Within a close enough proximity for his pleasure, but far enough away perhaps that she would not interact with his wife and children.

Yes. Eloise was exactly the sort of woman who would play mistress to a wealthy married man.

It would suit her. She had the cheekbones for it. Among other things.

He rang the doorbell. And there was no response.

Perhaps she was out.

He took a step off the path and around to the side of the house, checking for signs of life.

It was not a terribly secure property, and if nothing else, perhaps he would let himself in and see what information he could gather about Eloise and her current situation.

When he went around the side of the house, he heard a small sound.

It was… Humming.

Tuneless, rather terrible humming.

He paused and listened. He could not make out what the tune was, as it was just so sporadic and tone-deaf.

But there was something strangely charming about the cheer that seemed injected into the sound. And that was deeply strange as he could not remember being charmed by much of anything, least of all something cheerful. Not in his entire life.

When he rounded the corner, he was shocked by what he saw. The back of the most luscious figure he had seen in… He could not remember how long. The woman was bent over, working on something in the garden, and the trousers that she was wearing conformed to her ass in an extremely pleasing way. She stood, and he saw that the woman had wide hips, a narrow waist, and he was terribly hungry to see the front of her.

His second thought was that he had the wrong house. Because the Eloise he knew had that sort of gaunt, haunted look that her mother had, the hungry look of a woman who cared more to be attractive in photographs than in person. More angles than curves.

This must be the gardener, but if there was a gardener for the house then what had they been doing all this time? The place was wild as far as he could tell. He preferred things manicured and tightly kept. And this… Well, it was not.

The humming suddenly stopped. And the woman jumped, startled as if she sensed that she was being watched, and she turned. Her blue eyes went round, and her mouth dropped open. She was holding a potted plant, with a cheerful red blossom on the top. And then she dropped it, and the pottery shattered on the stones below.

"Vincenzo."

# CHAPTER TWO

ELOISE COULD NOT stop the flutter of her foolish, traitorous heart. This was like a dream. Like every shameful dream she prayed wouldn't be there waiting for her at night when she fell asleep, but always was.

For she had never forgotten him.

The man with the dark, compelling eyes, who made her feel things that no other man ever had. Who had awakened a desire inside of her when she was only fifteen years old and had held her in thrall ever since. Even though her seduction attempt had ended in a refusal, all these years later she could understand it in a way an eighteen-year-old hadn't, the memory of the one and only time she had ever been close enough to touch him still lingered in her mind and made her tremble in her sleep.

But that wasn't her worst memory of Vincenzo. Her most painful. No. It had been the way he'd sent her away. The way he'd believed... Everything.

Everything except what she'd told him.

She'd been so certain they'd been friends. That he'd cared for her.

But that final moment between them…

He'd made it clear he'd never really cared for her at all.

Did that stop her body from responding to the steamy visions of him that floated through her subconscious at night?

No. No, it did not.

He occupied her dreams. He occupied her fantasies…

He was currently occupying her garden.

"Eloise," he said.

And she could see that he… He had not known it was her.

She was vaguely embarrassed by that, but only for a moment. Because she was accepting of the shape that her body had taken in the years since she had left the palace. She liked the changes in herself. The changes that had occurred when she could finally control her own life. When she could decide what her priorities were. When she no longer had to live beneath the shadow of her mother and her impossible standards.

Still, it was always vaguely hurtful to realize that you were so different you were not even recognizable.

"Yes," she said. "Quite. But you… You cannot be here by accident. Because this house is not on the way to anything, least of all anything that you would be headed to."

"Indeed it is not," he said, sliding his dark jacket from his broad shoulders and casting it onto a white chair that boasted intricate iron scrollwork, with one careless finger. It seemed a metaphor for his existence here. The very masculine object covering the delicate, feminine one.

He turned his wrist and undid the button on his cuff, rolling his sleeve up and revealing a muscular forearm before doing the same to the right side. She blinked, watching with deep interest. Interest that she tried not to feel. And definitely tried not to convey.

"Why are you here?"

His dark eyes met with hers and her heart slammed against her breastbone. He was still the perfect image of masculine beauty. And she feared that for her he always would be. The way his tanned skin gleamed in the sunlight, that same light catching in his dark eyes and displaying a dangerous fire there. She had always thought his eyes so compelling. They were so dark they were nearly black, and she wanted to get lost in the depths of them.

She had embarrassed herself horribly as a teenager staring at him, or at least, she would've liked to embarrass herself horribly staring at him. But he had never noticed. He had practically acted as if she was invisible. Again, with hindsight, she was grate-

ful for that, and had she not horrifically misstepped
he would probably never have noticed her at all.

But she had.

And she felt covered in shame about it even all
these years later. That she'd believed she loved him.
That she'd believed he loved her.

*No. Forgive yourself. Forgive her.*

She did try.

She had tried to change her life entirely. Step away
from the path her mother had wanted her to be on.
To find out who Eloise St. George was all on her
own. Not a girl living in the palace and the shadow
of her mother's great and terrible beauty. Not a girl
who had been taught that the only value she had was
in her beauty. That girl who had believed, in spite
of all that, she might really find a fairy tale. When
she'd left Arista, it had been under a cloud of shame.
Every newspaper in the world printing lies about her
and touting them as verified truths.

It had hurt her. Profoundly. As had Vincenzo's belief in them. But when she'd gone, when she'd found
life outside the palace… Away from her mother, his
father and Vincenzo himself…

She'd gained perspective. She'd realized how
many things had been built up in that palace that
simply weren't real. Her mother's ideals had no bearing on the life she lived out here, in the sunshine,
amongst the flowers. The King's gaze didn't follow
her here, and while the press might have tried to

ensure she had no real peace or opportunity to get
work, enough time had passed—and she'd managed
to make for herself a good reputation in her field and
she'd never struggled to get work.

Reality was rich and deep and warm away from
the cold stone of Arista.

It felt like an illusion now.

Parts of it.

One thing she was confident in was that her feelings for Vincenzo had been real. They had not been
based in a desire to snare herself a rich protector.
They had not been about anything other than the
fact that he had captured her from the moment she
had first laid eyes on him at six years old. As silly
as that was. Of course, back when she had been a
child, there had been nothing sexual about it; it was
simply that she had found him... Wonderful. There
was something about him that reminded her of a
knight in shining armor.

He had been kind to her. One of her few experi-
ences of kindness. And in her memory, in spite of
how things had ended between them, he was still
that mythological figure.

But the way he was looking at her now...

There was nothing heroic about it. And she was
quite certain that he had not come to save her.

*You don't need to be saved.*

"I'm here to take you back with me, Eloise." He
did not look away from her, his dark gaze unwaver-

ing. Her chest went tight, her throat. She could feel her insides trembling.

"To Arista?"

Thinking of Arista, of returning there made her feel cold inside. And why he would want her to come back when he'd paid her to go away in the first place...

"Yes," he said.

"Vincenzo... Has something happened to your father...? Or my mother...?"

"No," he said. "But I require you, for a very specific purpose. You will not be returning with me in whatever capacity you might imagine. You see, you are an important instrument in my revenge against my father."

She blinked. "I am?"

"Yes," he said. "And I think you will find that there is sufficient reason for you to return with me. Whether you wish to or not."

"Vincenzo," she said, trying to force a smile, because after all, they had been a part of each other's lives for a great number of years, and there was no reason to be grim. "If you need my help, you have only to ask."

And she couldn't say then what was driving her. She could tell herself it was that she cared for him, whatever had passed between them. She could tell herself it was because she wanted to do something to ease the darkness coming off him in waves.

But what she did not tell herself was that it had anything to do with the tendrils of pleasure that curled around her stomach when she thought of revenge.

He made a compelling picture. A dark avenging angel standing before her, asking her to indulge her basest self.

*You don't own that pain. That rage, none of it is yours. You let it go.*

She breathed in deep and smelled the lilacs.

And thought of vengeance still. If only a little.

"I have only to ask?"

She forced a smile. "Of course. I'm sure that we can discuss whatever it is you're planning. There's no reason for you to come here all dark and angry and threatening. No reason to threaten me at all. Can you go over there to the shed?"

"I'm sorry?"

"To the shed. My broom is in there. And you made me break my plant."

"*You* broke your plant," he said.

"Yes," she said, feeling slightly testy. "But it was because you startled me. So would you be so kind as to get my broom."

"Perhaps you have forgotten who I am?"

"I haven't. You're the one who didn't seem to know who I was. I said your name immediately. How could I fail to recognize you? I could not. Ever. And I think you know that. Please get my broom."

"And…"

"And then we will discuss your plot."

"It is not a plot."

"It sounds like a plot to me. Complete with intrigue. Vincenzo, I am no great fan of your father, neither am I particularly fond of my mother. There is a reason that I have not been back to Arista in all these years. Depending on what you have in mind… I will help you."

"Just like that?"

She hesitated "Of course."

"I will get your broom, and then you will explain to me what you've been doing this past decade and a half."

"Oh, a great many things," she said, trailing behind after him as he went to the shed.

He opened the door, and fished around inside until he grabbed a broom. "Why did you follow me if you sent me on the errand? You could've easily retrieved the thing yourself."

"Yes, I suppose," she said. "I didn't mean to follow you. It just sort of happened. But I am intrigued. What has happened? What are your plans?"

"Nothing more has happened than what has been happening in my country ever since my father ascended to the throne. He is corrupt. He has kept your mother in secret as his mistress while masquerading for all the world as an overbearing, pious leader who has inflicted a false morality upon the entire country that he himself is not held to. I, as you know, am his great public shame, and yet what he's done to my mother over the years is unconscionable. I will expose it. And I will do so by making a public display that will destroy him."

Hearing him say those words, while omitting any mention of her made her breathless and a bit dizzy. "And what do I have to do with it?"

"I may not approve of you, Eloise, but the fact is my father's…dalliance with you is another example of why he must be dealt with. Only you were ever hurt by it, not him. Do you not find that unfair?"

Even more unfair, considering she'd never touched him. And never would.

But the truth hadn't mattered to the press.

Or to Vincenzo.

"Life is not fair, Vincenzo, or did no one ever tell you that?"

"I aim to balance the scales. By taking everything he has."

His dark eyes glittered with a black flame, and an answering heat smoldered in her stomach, but she did not allow that to show.

Instead, she scrunched up her nose, looking up at him, backlit as he was by the sun. "That does all sound a bit intense. I don't suppose you've ever tried therapy?"

"Therapy," he repeated, his voice flat, the broom still in his hand, which was an incongruous sight.

She had to wonder if Vincenzo had ever held a broom before. She did not imagine he had.

"Yes. I have found it incredibly helpful. I no longer get angry. Now I garden."

"You garden."

"Yes," she said. "Of course, now I have one less flower." She took the broom from his hand and went back over to the scene of its destruction. "But that doesn't matter. I can always plant more. That is the wonderful thing about nature. It is incredibly resilient. It grows, and it thrives, often in spite of us. I find it quite cheering. Bettering myself is one of my pursuits since leaving Arista. But only one of them. I went to school for horticulture. I made a lot of friends. I traveled around. I…"

"With my money?"

Heat lashed at her. "You gave it to me."

"I paid you off."

"Did you want revenge on me? Or on your father."

"It is only that you speak of those accomplishments as if they are yours when we both know how you paid for them."

"Do not look at me like that," she said. "How is it that you've managed to finance your life?"

"I have made my own way."

"From the starting position of 'billionaire prince,'" she said. "Your father, your lineage, gave you your start in life. I had to… I had to make the best of what I was given. I will not apologize for it."

His appraisal of her was decisive and cold, and she felt as if it had cut her down to her bones. "I don't require your apology."

"And I don't require your approval, so now we have that out of the way, what is it you want from me?"

"It's simple," he said, and she did not like the way he said that. Simplicity for a man with the sort of power and bearing Vincenzo Moretti possessed meant nothing to mere mortals such as herself.

*Simple* could mean flying a private jet to an equally private island, or rallying the whole of the media to listen to him speak. It could be climbing a ladder to collect stars from the sky.

Simple for Eloise was something else entirely. An evening at home with a cup of tea, or an afternoon in the garden.

Definitely without her mother in her vicinity.

He was looking at her. As if "it's simple" was all she needed to know.

"If 'simple' involves reading your mind, you have the wrong idea of 'simple.'"

"It's not a negotiation," he said. "Nor am I asking for your help, I'm demanding you come with me. I see no reason to continue to speak in your garden."

"I said I would help you. You can stop looming so menacingly." She turned on her heel and stalked toward the house, throwing the back door open and going inside.

It was warm.

There was no air conditioner, and by late afternoon not even the stones could keep the heat at bay. But she didn't mind it. It was hers. And, all right, Vincenzo might dispute that, because she had taken that horrible money he'd flung at her to run away and had used some to purchase this house. But it felt like hers. It felt like home. And she'd been the happiest here than she'd been anywhere.

And yet he made her feel like she had one foot back in that life again.

*You agreed to help him...*

But she knew him.

The threats were not empty, and she wouldn't win if she argued. And if she didn't choose to go with him, she would be forced to go.

One thing Eloise could not bear, not ever again, was to have her choice taken away. And in this instance she knew she could change it, retain her power.

She had shocked him with her easy offer to help.

She wanted to keep shocking him.

She had spent her life in the palace at Arista on the defense. She had been out of place in every way. Her mother had always been a hard woman, who saw Eloise as an accessory to play dress-up with when it suited her, and a doll to discard when it did not.

The King had not paid any attention to her, until he had.

And Vincenzo? He'd been her only ally.

Until he wasn't.

"I will have to pack. And I need to see if my neighbor can feed Skerret."

His brow creased. "What is…that?" he asked.

"My cat. Well, she's not my cat entirely. She looms around the garden—a lot like you, actually—and I feed her."

He arched one dark brow, his expression beautifully insolent. "You have not fed me. Should I be offended?"

"Likely." But she was busy texting her neighbor Paula to see if she could leave food for the poor little tabby while she was away.

Paula responded with a quick yes. And when she looked back up at Vincenzo, it was because she could feel the impatience radiating off him in palpable waves.

"There is a breathing exercise I learned," she said. "It helps with tension."

"You are not my therapist."

"You don't have a therapist," she said. "I think we already covered that."

"No, I do not. But when we get back to Arista… you will be playing the part of my mistress."

Her mouth dropped open and she couldn't help it. She laughed.

"Your *what*?" She couldn't stop laughing. She

laughed so hard tears streamed down her face, because he could not be serious.

To her great shame she had followed his... Trajectory, she would call it, for the last ten years. She had seen him in the news with an endless parade of women. All perfect. All gorgeous. All... Very not her.

"I do not believe I said anything that was difficult to comprehend."

"Oh, no, I comprehend, I just think you're way off. There is no way anyone would believe that I was your mistress."

"The world is unaware of *our* complicated history, *cara*."

*Cara.* He had never called her that. She had heard him call other women that, though. He used to bring them to the palace, after ostentatiously arriving in the country with them on his arm.

She could remember the fury of his father—always—when he had done so.

*He is a disgrace.*

*Trying to humiliate me.*

*Trying to diminish the Crown.*

She wondered now if he had been. All along. If Vincenzo had truly set out to tarnish the institution from day one.

But mostly the word *cara* echoed inside of her and made her feel light-headed.

She shook it off. "They are all too aware of..."

"Your affair with my father? That is why I want you. You were made to take all the scorn upon yourself. An eighteen-year-old temptation no man could resist." His dark eyes went blank, and she was glad. She'd defended herself already back then; she wouldn't keep doing it. But hearing him repeat the things the tabloids had said wasn't easy.

"Why bring me back?"

"A triumphant return, Eloise. On my arm. A reminder of when his mask slipped, and then we will tear it off together. We will force the reality of truth upon the masses. These are different times. Even I have changed in how I see things. A man of his age has a certain power. A man of his position more still. You were an eighteen-year-old girl and for all that I disapproved…you were given sole blame. I think if the world is forced to look at it in this new time they would see him for what he is. A predator with no morals."

He wasn't wrong. Things had changed. Too late for her, but they had.

"But why would anyone believe you're with me?"

"I'm a man of great debauchery—no one will find it hard to believe I've taken on my father's former… You."

"No, that's not what I mean."

She stared at him and waited for him to figure it out. He only stared back. Enigmatic and hard, like a sheer cliff face.

"Are you going to make me say it, Vincenzo? Because I knew you were a bastard, but I thought being deliberately cruel to me might be a bit beneath you."

"Explain to me how I am being cruel?"

"I am not beautiful. Not by the standards those people use to measure it. And sample sizes are hardly going to fit this figure."

He laughed. He dared laugh! That dark chuckle rolling through her like a lick of flame. "Sample sizes? *Cara*, I am not your mother. I do not need to debase myself bargain hunting. Whatever I provide for you will be fitted especially to your exquisite curves."

*"Exquisite?"* She had never been called anything even adjacent to *exquisite*. "I am not your type," she said.

"Beautiful? Lush? Beddable? That is not my type?"

He said it as if he were reciting a shopping list.

Milk.

Bread.

Beddable.

*Beddable*. She couldn't get over *that*.

"I am round," she said, her voice flat.

"Lush," he said, his voice far too seductive. "The narrow view on beauty your mother fed you…"

"To be clear," she bit out. "I am not insecure. I like my life. I like my body. As much as I like cookies. But I do not want to subject myself to what will undoubtedly be a heap of criticism from the press. I have been there and I've done it all before. And this time I know exactly what they'll do. With glee. Don't you think they'll put photos of me side by side and speculate on my weight gain?"

"But you are not eighteen," he said, his voice fierce. "And you will not run this time."

"You mean I will not be banished?"

"Let us go."

"I should pack a bag."

"You will want for nothing. By the time we arrive at the plane, a seamstress and a rack of clothing will be there waiting. You will be fitted and the items altered en route to Arista. By the time we arrive, you will look every inch mine."

*Mine.*

She shivered.

Then she shook it off.

This was not a fantasy. He might be a prince, but in this case she had a feeling he was less knight in shining armor, and more the dragon who might eat her alive.

# CHAPTER THREE

ELOISE SEEMED TO have a personal mission of being unexpected. He had expected her to do one of two things when he had demanded she go with him: to cry hysterically and call him a brute before ultimately capitulating to his blackmail. Or to flirt while succumbing to his bribery.

She did neither.

Instead she had looked up at him with round eyes and a seeming lack of artifice and had said she would help him.

She reminded him more of the girl he'd known than the woman he'd made her into in his mind when he'd discovered her association with his father.

But now he wondered if she'd changed in that moment, or if he had. And it was a discomfiting thought.

Even now as they boarded his private plane, comfortably fitted with many rooms and all the amenities a person could ever want, she looked… She did not look *bored*, or as if she was stepping into her due. Rather she had an expression on her face of a woman who was surprised and delighted by her surroundings.

Perhaps *delighted* was an overstatement. But there was something fascinated in her gaze, and it was not the sort of bright avarice that he might've expected with a woman such as her. No. It seemed to be more interest.

Enjoyment.

There was a purity to her response that... Took him off guard. For he had never applied the concept of *purity* to Eloise St. George.

"Is there something you wish to say?" he asked as he settled onto the soft leather sofa in the main seating area of the aircraft.

"Only that it's quite grand," she responded. "The plane."

"It is to my advantage to have everything well in its place for when I travel. I must be able to function as if I were in my own home."

"Well naturally," she said. "It must be so horribly taxing for you to travel to and fro as you do. I myself have been quite stagnant for much of my life. Though, of course my mother enjoyed traveling with your father on occasion. And sometimes I went too. A testament to your father's great kindness," she said, the words biting. "That he would bring not only his assistant, but her child. But his plane is not quite so spectacular."

"Indeed not," Vincenzo said.

He could not quite figure out what game she was playing, and that caused him a hint of concern. Concern was a foreign feeling, as was the sense that he could not read another person.

He *knew* plenty enough about Eloise. A mere week after she'd come to *his* room—tried to seduce him. Told him she loved him, kissed him—the story had broken about her affair with his father.

And he'd... Well he'd considered himself a saint for sending her away. Desire had been a living, breathing beast inside of him and even then he'd known. She was far too young. And most importantly, she would barely remember life away from the palace. They had grown up together, and in some ways they'd grown up alone.

She'd thought she loved him because she was too innocent to know better.

And so he'd told her no. Told her they couldn't...

What a fool he'd been. An even bigger fool for the pain he'd felt when he'd discovered that she had never loved him—she only wanted to align herself with a crown.

And any would do.

He had learned. He had learned since then to harden himself.

"Have a drink," he said.

As soon as he said those words, his stewardess

appeared and walked over to the bar. "What would the lady like?" she asked.

"Oh," Eloise said. "A club soda would be nice."

"A club soda," he said. "Please do not hesitate to put a larger dent in my bar than that."

"I don't often drink."

It surprised him. For he had imagined…

He had imagined a whole woman in his head that it seemed did not exist. And that was what he was finding here.

He had imagined Eloise sharp and pointed, like her mother. Had imagined her with heavy makeup and a daring taste in clothing. He had thought she would feign boredom at his plane, consume his entire bar and demand to know how she would be compensated for all of this time spent inconvenienced.

But she looked different. Spoke different. Acted different.

He was certain he was rarely wrong, and yet with her, it seemed he was.

"If you are saving it for a special occasion, then let us make this one. For we are rather triumphantly returning back to Arista, are we not?"

"I don't know that I find it triumphant to return to Arista."

He waved a hand and his stewardess poured two glasses of champagne. She brought them over on a tray and he took them both, before handing one to Eloise, who stared at the fizzing liquid blinking rapidly.

"You do not feel triumphant, Eloise? You are... A horticulturist with a... I suppose it is what passes for a home in some circles. Do you not feel pleased with yourself?"

He found himself waiting. Waiting for the truth of her to be revealed. And it was a strange thing, he acknowledged to himself, that he had not done exhaustive research on her before he had gone to look for her. For in most circumstances he would've walked into the situation already knowing all the answers. He would have made sure that he had them. But he had been so certain that Eloise St. George could not surprise him. That she was the exact same tawdry, sparkling bit of cloth that her own mother was, and cut right from it. Why should he do research?

"Nothing that I am is designed to make my mother proud," Eloise said, lifting the champagne to her lips. She looked somewhat surprised when the liquid touched her tongue, and he had to confess that either she was a very good actress, or she truly did not often drink.

He was leaning toward her being a very good actress.

"You know how I feel about her," she said softly.

"I thought I did," he said. "But then, I thought I knew you once."

"I never lied, Vincenzo," she said softly, "whatever you might think."

Her eyes were sincere, and this woman sitting in front of him was...

She was not a surprise.

He had created a fictional Eloise in his head because he had wanted to banish all images of the girl he'd once cared for. Had fashioned her into a mold that would make it easy for him to do that. The same mold as her mother.

But if...

If that night, when she'd kissed him. When he'd held her in his arms for a brief moment before sending her away. If he'd imagined who she might become then, he might have seen the person sitting before him.

He hardened himself. For that was a nice thought, but it was all it was. And he knew well how adept some people could be at fooling the masses, and while he had never fancied himself a member of said masses, he knew that Eloise had tricked him once.

He would not allow her to do it again.

"Lies. Truth. None of it matters now."

"It does to me. I don't enjoy sitting with a man who despises me."

"And yet you have agreed to help me. Why would you do that if you did not wish to return? Why would you do that if you hate me so?"

"I never said I hated you."

His gaze flickered over her, and her cheeks went pink. His blood warmed. "You should."

"Why? Because you hate me? It doesn't work that way."

"I don't hate you, Eloise. If I hated you, I would have done this without you. What I want to know is the manner of your investment in this."

"I have always thought..." She did not look at him; rather she looked over the top of her champagne glass, straight ahead at the back wall of the plane. "We were not so different, Vincenzo. Your father does not care for you any more than my mother cares for me. We are simply caught in the middle of their games. That was why we were able to become friends. Me, a girl from America who didn't even know princes existed outside of fairy tales...and you, the heir to a country. I care for you. It was only that friendship that carried me through. And so I would happily act as your friend now."

The word cut him.

*"Friends,"* he repeated.

"Please don't embarrass me," she said, her voice going tight. "Please do not bring it up."

It was anger that drove him now and he felt a sick shame with it. He was better than this. Better than the sort of man who was led around by emotion. Better than his father. And yet he couldn't help himself. "Are you speaking of our last encounter, when I sent you away, or of the night when you were eighteen and you..."

He looked up at his stewardess and gestured for

her to leave the room. The woman stared for a moment, then caught herself before retreating to the staff's quarters.

He turned his eyes back on Eloise. "The night when you threw yourself at me with quite the brazen…"

"Oh, yes, I was so very brazen," she said, her tone tart. "Kissing you with all that experience of mine and crying and saying I loved you."

In some ways he was surprised that she even remembered it. And he had to wonder what the purpose of bringing it up now was. But he would've brought it up, she was correct. So perhaps using it against him before he could use it against her was the game.

"It is a vague memory for me," he lied. "Any number of women fling themselves at me, Eloise, and you were simply one more."

She looked wounded, and for a moment he regretted landing the blow. For the pain in her blue eyes did not seem to be manufactured. And if it was, she had manufactured it quite quickly and had managed to cover any sort of shock she might be experiencing.

"All for the best, then," Eloise said, taking another sip of champagne. She sat down on the couch, her feet—clad in white sneakers—pressed tightly together, along with her knees. Her shoulders seemed to be contracted, as if she was trying to shrink in on herself.

He took the moment to look at her. Really look at her. She had a red handkerchief tied around her head, her blond hair tucked into an old-fashioned-looking roll. She was wearing a bright blue button-up shirt knotted at the waist, trimmed to accentuate her full bust and small midsection. The pants she wore were red like her handkerchief and cuffed at the ankles. She looked like a 1950s pinup waiting to happen. All he would have to do was unfasten the top few buttons of her blouse. No doubt her cleavage was abundant. It was a shame that it was done up all the way so that he could not see it.

And it bothered him. Bothered him that he was sitting there counting buttons and trying to gauge how many it would take to reveal her glory.

She was subtle. She had no makeup on today, but her skin was bright and clear, her eyes that pale cornflower blue. Her lips a pale pink, full, the top lip rounded and slightly fuller than the bottom.

He remembered that.

The color of her eyes, the shape of her mouth. But her face had been much narrower then, while now it had rounded. Her cheekbones were high and elegant, but not razor-sharp, and he found the new arrangement of her features pleasing.

He could not think of any man who would not.

The truth was, she was an entirely lovely creature. He had been prepared to resist the creature he had made her into in his mind. He had not been prepared to confront the woman she was.

But it might be a ruse. "Tell me, what are your current entanglements?"

"My…entanglements?"

"Lovers. Employers."

"I'm a horticulturist. Though I am between jobs at the moment."

"Between jobs?" He could not work out if she was speaking euphemistically or not.

"I was working at a large estate up until last month. But the owner sold it, and…" She closed her eyes, as if the memory was painful. "The greenhouse that I was in charge of curating was done away with. It was quite a lot of work. Had some beautiful mature plants, all gone now so that someone can have a new pool area. I had enough money that it was not immediately necessary for me to get more work. So I've been considering starting my own nursery. I haven't gotten that far. But it is something that I'm in the early stages of planning."

He could not help himself. He wanted to know… Why? He kept trying to remember if she had particularly liked plants and flowers back when he'd known her and could not recall that she had. "And why horticulture? Why are you invested in that particular vocation?"

"I just like the idea of growing things. Of leaving the world a little bit more beautiful. I actually don't want to be notorious. And you know… It doesn't really matter if I am. For I will just fade back into obscurity. I will go back to the garden. It doesn't matter to me. I want to be able to live on my own terms. I know you might not believe that, but it's true. My mother controlled everything in my life. What I thought, what I did, what I ate, what I wore. And I like being myself. I like leaving the world fuller, rather than simply taking from it."

She was not going to answer his question, then. And he had to wonder if the person who owned the manor house she had previously worked at had also been her paramour. That would make sense. That she had not simply lost her job, but been removed as his mistress. Perhaps she was in between lovers then.

She seemed to have little concern for money, and while he knew that she had been given some money by his father, and she had presumably been earning money at her job, he could not credit that it was enough to truly support her.

Especially not in the lifestyle she would...

But he was forced to look at her again and ask himself what lifestyle she was truly paying for.

Well, he did not need to itemize the cost of her clothing. She was in an outfit that she had been gardening in. That was not a true reflection of her life. And just because the woman liked to dig in the dirt did not make her truly unexpected.

"Are you finished with your champagne?"

"I suppose."

"Let us go for your fitting."

"My fitting?"

"I told you, that you would be fitted here on the plane."

"Oh, yes, but I…"

"All of the clothing is in my study. Along with the seamstress."

"I don't even know what to say to that. That feels a great amount of excess. Being fitted thirty thousand feet above ground."

"We have not reached cruising altitude yet."

She blinked. "Indeed."

He walked over to where she was and extended a hand. She looked up at him as though it were a shark.

"You must be comfortable with my touch."

Her eyes went round. "Must I?" He had the distinct feeling he was being mocked.

"You must *appear* to be," he amended.

She squinted, then took hold of his hand, and the contact of her soft skin against his was like a punch to the gut.

How he would like her hands to be wrapped around other parts of him.

It would be helpful if he could think of her as dowdy. But he was a man with far too much experience of the female form to look at that outfit and not understand exactly what she would look like naked. How she would appear when the layers of her clothing were stripped away.

She was not dowdy at all.

She was the embodiment of sex. Sex he would like to have. Quite a lot. And that outraged him.

He'd thought he would be immune to her now.

He was… He held on to his memories of that moment finding out she'd been with his father so that he would keep her at a distance. It should not be so easy for her to make him want her.

It should not be so easy for him to forget.

When they walked into the study, her eyes went even rounder than they'd been previously. "This is incredible," she said. "I had no idea that a private plane could be quite so… It is a palace unto itself."

"Yes. As I told you. I spend quite a bit of time flying."

There was a rack of gowns and a smooth, immaculate man ready to do his bidding.

He went to his desk and sat on the chair. "Begin," he said.

"You cannot possibly… You cannot possibly expect me to undress in front of you," she said.

Why was she so modest now? She had climbed into bed with him once, her thighs on either side of his as she'd kissed him earnestly, and now she didn't want to undress in front of him?

*Do you want her to?*

"You may lower your dander," he said. "There is a screen for you to step behind. But I will be approving each and every gown. So I will be here the entire time."

It turned out that the entire experience was an exercise in torture.

He had not intended to dress her subtly. And so the gowns that had been provided by Luciano were not subtle in the least. Gold and glittering, bright and tight. Creative shapes designed to accentuate curves, and cutouts that flirted dangerously with revealing parts of her body that only a lover should see.

"I…" She looked at herself in the mirror, and her face contorted with shock. She was currently in a gold gown with a deep V at the front, exposing the rounded curves of her breasts. The back was low, and the vision of the two dimples that he knew were just above her rounded ass was making him hard.

"This is far too revealing," she said.

"Are you uncomfortable?"

"I am."

"Do you think you look bad?" He felt the need to comfort her, and he could not untangle his feelings for her.

He was not a man who trafficked in uncertainty, and he hated this. Not enough to be cruel to her. Not now.

"Women of my shape do not wear dresses like this," she said.

"And why is that?"

"I am a strong breeze away from a wardrobe malfunction, and that's just the first issue. The second is that it's… Clearly made for a runway-ready sort of woman, and not…"

"Runways are changing, or have you not noticed?"

Her cheeks went pink and he wondered if he had said the wrong thing. In his opinion, the change was welcome. He was the sort of man who liked variety. To him, these changes were only good.

"It does not matter if they are changing," she said. "I would still be a novelty, not the accepted. I will be in the same room as my mother and I will look like…"

"You will look like what?" She had been confident and happy when he'd taken her from the garden, freely offering herself to his revenge, and he could see her changing before his eyes.

As if the closer they were to her mother, the further she was from her confidence.

When he'd decided she was a liar, he'd decided everything about her was a lie.

Their friendship. Her relationship with her mother. Her feelings for him.

What if some of it were true?

"I think it's fierce," Luciano said. "For what it's worth."

Eloise grimaced. "I… I appreciate that. But I do not feel fierce. I feel… Round."

"You say that as if it is a bad shape," Vincenzo said.

"Do not play dense," she said. "When I think you

know that hip bones are much more de rigueur than hips."

"I understand that it is your mother's preference, but that has little bearing on the truth of actual beauty. It is not so narrow, I feel. And who are you trying to impress? Your mother? As you said yourself, she recognizes only a very specific thing. But I wish to show you to the world, and I guarantee you that your sex appeal will not be missed."

"People will compare. And they will comment."

"Perhaps. But I am your lover," he said, the words making his gut tight, increasing the flow of blood down south of his belt. "And I find you glorious. If Luciano were not here I would strip the gown off you and lay you down on the floor."

He intended it to be a performance. Establishing the connection between the two of them, but it felt all too real. It felt all too much like the truth.

He drew closer to her, and he had not meant to. She smelled…

The same.

And it took him back.

To the girl she'd been.

Worse still, to the boy he'd been.

He leaned in, as he traced a line from her neck down across her bare shoulder. And he whispered in her ear.

"And I would have you screaming my name inside of thirty seconds. That is what I see when I look at that dress."

And he forgot. Why they were here. And that it was now.

And that he was supposed to keep her at arm's length.

There was no distance between them now.

She turned scarlet. From the roots of her pale hair, down all the glorious curves of her body.

"I just… I just wonder if there is perhaps a more subtle way to accomplish this."

"I have an idea," Luciano said.

He took an emerald green gown off the rack and handed it to her.

She went behind the screen, and when she appeared, she was somehow all the more maddeningly beautiful. The gown was crushed velvet, off the shoulder and conformed itself to her curves, while not revealing overly much skin. It was tight all the way down to her knees, then flared out around her feet.

"This I like," she said.

"It will do," he said, keeping himself away from her this time. "But fit the gold one to her as well. And use the rest of the measurements to fit some casual clothes too."

"I like a retro style," she said.

"I have a good handle on your style based on the outfit you had on today," said Luciano. "The gowns will be ready by the time we land, and the rest of the items should be there within a day. I will call ahead to my studio and have my staff get to work."

"Thank you," he said. "You may get dressed," he said to Eloise.

"Oh, may I?"

"Yes."

"May I also use the bathroom?" she asked, disappearing behind the screen.

"You do not need a hall pass."

"It's only that I thought I might."

She appeared a moment later, dressed again, but still tying her shirt up at her waist, and he wanted to round the desk, step toward her, hook his finger through the knot and undo it. Then undo all the rest of the buttons. Sadly, Luciano was still in the room, and also, he was never going to touch her in that way. Not for purposes other than performance.

*It is perverse*, he thought. And in some ways… Expected. He was a royalty, and very little was forbidden to him. So of course the luscious apple he should not take a bite of was the one he craved most of all.

She scampered out of the room then, and he thanked Luciano before leaving. She had used the closest bathroom, and he waited outside the door for her to appear. When she did, she nearly ran into him, her cheeks going red.

"Let me show you to your room. Where I think you will find the lavatory much more to your liking."

"I don't see anything wrong with that one."

"You might like a bath," he said.

"Oh, might I?"

"Yes. Are you intent upon being angry about all that I offer? May I remind you that you did come of your own accord."

"Yes," she said. "I did. Because I could not stand the idea of someone controlling my life yet again. It is something I cannot bear. And so I made the decision to come back with you. It was easier. It was better. Better than… Better than the alternative."

Guilt, which was an emotion he was entirely unaccustomed to, lanced his gut. She was tearing him in pieces. With memories. Memories that challenged his certainty.

And with herself. All that she was, and no matter what he knew about her, it didn't seem to matter. Didn't seem to keep him from wanting her.

He gritted his teeth and gestured down the hall, toward a glossy mahogany door. "This is you," he said.

He opened the door to reveal an expansive suite with a large, plush bed. He knew for a fact that the bathroom was ornate and very comfortable. He also knew that if he stepped in there, he would be tempted to invite her to draw a bath that included him.

And he did not like this feeling of being off-kilter. He could not afford it. Not now.

"I shall perhaps need you to explain to me what it is you expect," she said.

She looked vulnerable. She looked young. She looked like everything he knew she was not. And she absolutely did not look like her mother's daughter.

Was this how it happened? Was this how a woman sank her claws deeply into a man?

*No, that isn't fair and you know it.* Her mother's claws were not sunk into his father any more than his fangs were not sunk into her. They were together of their own accord, toxic of their own accord, and while Cressida St George had played havoc with his mother, his father happily engaged in hurting both of them.

"Rest," he said. "It is five hours yet before we land in Arista. We will go to my apartment first. Before we go to the palace."

She nodded. "All right."

"And we will engage the press."

She looked frightened, and he had to wonder if it was genuine. It seemed so.

"You needn't worry about instructions," he said. "You need only to follow me, and do as I say. And look at me as if I am the sun, the moon and the stars." And then he could not help himself. "You did so once."

"Yes," she said, her eyes suddenly filling with

tears. "But that night you barely remember knocked me out of the sky. And I have not tried to reach for the stars or the moon since."

Then she closed the door in his face and left him to wonder why his chest hurt.

# CHAPTER FOUR

SHE HAD A BATH, but she did not rest—it was impossible to rest, knowing that she was landing in Arista. Impossible to relax after what had happened...

She had made a fool of herself. She had exposed all of her insecurities. She was far too honest. She had reminded him of that night between them, one he said he didn't remember. *He didn't remember.*

She had loved Vincenzo Moretti more than anything. And she had never thought she would ever want a man. She hated the way her mother was with her lovers, and even though she'd only been six when they'd moved to Arista and her mother had taken up with the King, she could remember the men before.

She had told herself she would never let herself fall apart over men. That she would never depend on them. Vincenzo had always felt different.

She'd seen him as a friend first. A protector. By the time she was fifteen, her heart felt like it was going to pound out of her chest when he was near.

When he went away to school, coming back so rarely, she'd thought she would die.

She'd had no one, those lonely years, and she had lived for the times he would come home to visit. Which was why, when he graduated and came to Arista for a visit, she had decided to give herself to him.

To make sure he knew how much she loved him.

She'd been eighteen and, in spite of everything, full of hope.

She'd borrowed one of her mother's dresses that she'd never even worn. Tight and sexy and hopefully something that would capture his attention.

She'd sneaked into his room at midnight and he'd been in bed, shirtless. He'd been so beautiful her heart had caught in her throat. She'd nearly wept.

*"What are you doing here, Eloise?"*

*"I had to see you."*

*"You could have waited until breakfast."*

*"No. No, I couldn't."*

*She'd crossed the room and, with trembling limbs, climbed onto the bed, positioning her body over his. "I... I want you, Vincenzo. I love you."*

*She leaned down and kissed him. Her first kiss, and it was everything she'd ever wanted. Because it was him.*

*And for a moment, his hand went around to cradle the back of her head, and he kissed her back. She could feel him growing hard between her legs, and it sent a thrill through her body.*

*But then suddenly, he was pushing her away.*

*"Eloise, no. You are too young. You can't know what you want."*

*"I do know," she said, running her hands down his chest. "You. I want you. I love you."*

*"You don't know any other men. Go. Go away to school. Go away from here. Kiss other men. And if when you come back you think you love me still... You will always be my Eloise."*

But she wasn't. She hadn't been.

He'd been so quick to believe the lies his mother had told about her, that the press had told about her.

*"Go away from here, Eloise."*

*His face was like stone. "Vincenzo, I didn't... I would never."*

*"Take this." He held a check out in front of her. "Go and do not return."*

In the end, she thought perhaps she wasn't lovable.

Now of course she realized that was not the case. And she could not define herself by what the people around her could not or would not give. It was not her responsibility. She could only be true to herself. She could not take on the baggage of others; she could not make it about her. She'd had therapy. She knew that. But something about being around him made her feel eighteen again. Desperate to perform and do the right thing, and she hated it.

And the way he had looked at her...

Like he thought she was beautiful now. But she couldn't understand that. She didn't understand any of this.

When she went back into the bedroom, she was sure she was going to have to dress in the outfit she had come in, but to her surprise, a pair of soft white linen trousers and a white linen top had been laid out for her, along with a white lace bra and matching underwear.

It looked positively bridal, which was ridiculous, because he wasn't even pretending that they were to be married.

No, he was aiming to parade her before the world as his mistress. And she knew what he really thought of that. What that meant to him. It was exactly what he saw her mother as. And she did understand. They had both been traumatized by aspects of their lives, and she knew that.

It was just that... It was just that she despised how small this made her feel. It wasn't even her fear of the press. She had no remaining fear of them in truth. They'd already skinned her alive when she'd been a younger, more tender person.

It was how much it reminded her of being that needy, lonely girl, who wanted so badly to be whatever he might have wanted her to be. To be whatever her mother might've wanted her to be. She had become who Eloise wanted to be, and she was happy with that. Except…

Well, she had shut down the part of herself that wanted to be seen as attractive by men. The way that her mother was, the way that her mother had always been in those relationships concerned her. And what had happened with Vincenzo had worried her even more. Had convinced her that she could not be trusted to enter into that sort of relationship. And this only confirmed it, really. Because she was back to being insecure, back to feeling uncomfortable, back to being all of the things that she had tried to let go of. She was thinking about her body through the lens of other people, and she had determined to stop that.

*Are you thinking about it in terms of other people, or him?*

No. He had been… Complimentary.

The memory made her face warm.

There was a stern knock at the door, and she went to open it. And there he was, resplendent in a fresh dark suit, his black hair pushed off his forehead, his expression enigmatic.

He was far too much, this man. Perhaps he always had been. At any rate, he was far too much for her.

"We will begin our descent soon," he said. "Come and sit."

Her stomach tightened up, butterflies swirling around. Arista.

She had lived in America until she was six, until

her mother had met King Giovanni Moretti at a party where she had been with another man, and he had been with his wife. Up until then, Eloise had enjoyed a fairly comfortable life with a nanny who had cared a great deal for her.

She had not seen her mother often, but when she had it had been nice enough.

Then the King had brought them to Arista to live. And everything had changed. She had been turned into a secret. Isolated. Kept separate from the rest of the world. From friends. From everything.

Her palms felt sweaty. She had never thought that she would return to Arista. Being confident and healthy and happy was easy in Virginia. It was easy in the new life she had carved out for herself, which consisted of quiet evenings at home, gardening and monthly meetings with her flower arranging club. She had made for herself a quiet life with people who didn't know who she was. With people who didn't know who her mother was. With people who didn't have any idea what she had been like when she was younger. Where she had been headed.

But now she was going back to the scene of all she had been created to be, to her mother's barbs and his father's cold indifference.

Two yawning, empty corridors that recognized her loneliness and amplified it. Created an echo in her chest that expanded throughout her entire body.

She hated it. And she hated the idea of it even more.

*But what if he's right? What if this is your chance at redemption? Revenge.*

"You do not look well," Vincenzo commented as she sat down on the leather sofa.

"I am not," she said, shaking off her uncomfortable thoughts. "I don't enjoy the prospect of going back to Arista."

"You said you'd had therapy."

"I did. And it has all served me well far away from my mother and the site of all my trauma."

"Trauma?"

He asked the question with a faint hint of mocking to his tone, but she was past caring what he thought about anything. It didn't matter.

"Yes, I found life at the palace quite traumatic. Did you not?"

"I do not think in terms of my own trauma," he said, lifting his glass of whiskey to his lips.

"Can you say that you were happy there? Because it seems that you were away more than you were ever there. Unusual for the heir to the throne, don't you agree?"

"I will never take the throne. And I will never have an heir. It dies with me. It will be turned over to the people."

"Your father will be devastated by that."

His grin took on a wicked curve. "I hope so."

"Revenge," she said. "You did mention that."

"Do you not take any joy in this?"

She frowned, looking down at her hands. "I don't know. If I'm being honest with you, I don't know. I came with you, so maybe I… Maybe a part of me wants to hurt both of them. Maybe. I would hope not. I would hope that…"

"You would hope that you were somehow more enlightened than me while offering to come back as my friend and help me in my endeavors?"

"Yes," she said. "I'm sorry if you don't understand that. I'm not sure that I understand much of anything in regard to my own feelings right now."

"Something I never suffer from. But then, I believe that is because I am honest. I am honest about what I want. I am honest about who I am."

"And you don't believe that I am?"

He stared at her for a long moment. "You are many things, *cara*. I do not believe that honest is one of them. But you are beautiful. And you will make an excellent weapon to be wielded against my father, and that is all I require of you."

With those words settled like a brand in her breast, the plane touched down.

They were ushered into a car, and they began to drive on the narrow, cobbled roads that felt like a distant dream to her now.

A part of a person that she no longer acknowledged.

Eloise St. George.

Who wanted to be beautiful, like her mother. Who

wanted to be special. Who just wanted, and felt so hungry for whatever might make her feel whole. Feel real.

The approval of her mother.

The attention of Prince Vincenzo.

That poor girl. She did not know what love was.

*And you do now?*

She knew what it was not. She would accept that as progress.

"I never spent much time in the city," she said, looking out the window as they moved away from the small brick buildings into modern skyscrapers. The business district in Arista was as bright and modern as any other major city. It was only around the edges that the ancient charm of the place was still preserved.

"Of course, you wouldn't have."

"We would travel with your father's staff. We spent most of our time in Paris. I haven't been back to Paris since I was fifteen."

"Why not?"

"I told you. I have been living and working in Virginia. Do you think that I have the funds to be a jet-setter? I took the check you gave me and I made something from it. But it was hardly enough to make me independently wealthy for life. I am on a budget."

"And your many benefactors since have not flown you off to Europe?"

"My many benefactors? Do you mean my employers? Because no."

"No, I mean your *lovers*."

"What makes you assume I have lovers paying for my life?"

He stared at her for a long moment. "Are you telling me that you don't?"

The way he looked at her made her stomach feel tight.

"I'm not telling you anything," she said. "I am asking you a question. What about anything that I am, or any of my life you have seen, suggests to you that I have an endless array of sugar daddies trotting me about the globe?"

"It is only that your mother…"

"Yes. My mother. We are not the same. We don't look the same. We don't act the same. My mother has spent the last twenty years with your father. Living a strange half-life. They cheat on each other, of course. My mother takes other lovers. But still, she is a creature of the night, wandering around European cities after dark because she can never be connected to him. Because she cannot have the notoriety she would prefer. Because she must trade that in for money. The most glittering, celebrated, reviled socialite America had to offer way back at the turn of the millennium, and now she is obscure. That's who you think I am? An undercover piece on the side? Managing to stay out of the tabloids because I have taken up with someone so lofty that I am a secret? Or perhaps you imagine I am more of a common tart, and none of the men that I associate with need to be quite so careful of the press?"

It wasn't the first time people had assumed things about her because of her mother. There was no excuse for it, ever. She hated it. It made her feel small and grim and sad.

"You forget," he said, his tone dark. "You forget what we all know to be true."

"You think I'm a whore. Go ahead and say it."

It wouldn't be the first time one of the Moretti men had accused her of such.

"I assumed you had continued on in the lifestyle you'd begun at the palace."

"Because you think you know the truth? Because of something your mother told you? As if she had any reason to…as if she would have ever wanted you to like me, Vincenzo."

"Be careful what you accuse my mother of," he said, his teeth gritted.

"Why? She was not careful of what she accused me of. And even if it were true? Are you better than me?"

"Eloise…"

"No. Admit it. You are just like your father. Just like all those sorts of men. You think you can judge a woman by the way she dresses, and you think that you know her moral character based on the amount of men you think she might've slept with. That doesn't teach you anything about a woman. How many women have you slept with? And were they wealthy? You have paraded all around the globe with great glittering creatures on your arm. What am I to learn about your morals from that?"

He laughed. Bitter and hard-edged. "You mistake me. I never said that I was better. I never said that I was better than my father. Or than you. I am simply different. I hardly lead a life worth canonizing. Nor do I pretend to. I am steeped in all manner of immorality, and I have never acted differently. And that is the only real difference between myself and my father. That and the fact that my liaisons affect only me. And I will not seek to flex my power over my people. That, perhaps, is my only real redeeming feature. I am not power hungry. I have power. I find that with it, I am able to ignore any appetite for more. I have money. I am not afraid of losing my status. I know who I am. My father is small. He fears being deposed. He fears being unmasked. He fears that in the end all that he is, all that he cares for and all that he pretends to be will be unveiled. Will be destroyed. I will see that it is. As for me? There are no surprises. There is nothing to destroy. I have been working to restore Arista to its former glory behind the scenes for many years. I will give all that must be given to the country and its people. And yes, I will continue on as a whoremonger. But I will not enforce moral ity that I do not myself believe in upon my people. I will not put on a mask. You mistake me. I do not care what you do. I do not care who you have slept with. And I do not care who is bankrolling your life. Only that I do not wish to be lied to."

"You have not earned the right to my honesty," she said, her chest feeling tight. "I don't like to give people access to my secrets."

"And why is that?"

"Other than the fact the press already tried to make me a public commodity? Somewhere in the middle of your secrets, all your insecurities are buried. And what do people love more than anything else? To use those against you. I will not expose myself to such a thing. I will not make myself an easy target. I refuse. So I will not prostrate myself for the enjoyment of any man. Least of all you."

"So long as you're a good actress, I suppose in the end it doesn't matter."

He shifted, and she smelled the spicy scent of him. Her entire being fluttered.

The real concern was that she would not have to pretend at all to act as if she was attracted to him. The real concern was that she wore it with obvious ease.

The real concern was that anyone might know.

But most especially, him.

The car pulled up to the front of a grand building made entirely of glass and steel. The windows reflected the mountains in the distance, and the intensity and magnitude of it sucked the breath straight from her lungs. This was his palace. A palace so unlike the traditional palace where they would go later tonight. The deliberate flex of his distinct power was obvious here. He was younger. A man who had earned his money, not a man who had taken it out of the pockets of the citizens of Arista. They got out of the car, and the doors to the building opened automatically. The lobby was stunning. All modern architecture that gleamed with gold rather than the expected chrome. It was not ornate or tacky, rather there was something like fire about it that made the entire place burn hotter.

The doors to the elevator had that same gold, brushed bright. He put his fingerprint on a panel, and the doors opened.

"This is my private elevator. It is the only way to get to my suite of rooms."

"And so you have made yourself the King of Arista after all."

The back wall to the elevator faced the city, and as they rose high above the buildings, looking out over the expansive view, she could see what she said being proven. He had no rejoinder, because there was nothing to be said.

"All of our things will be sent soon. You may have a rest."

"I should like some food."

"We are having dinner at the palace."

"Yes. But by then I will have a stomach full of anxiety, and I would like something to eat."

He gestured across the barren, modern space. The floors were black, the counter cement. But yet again the details in gold. "Be my guest."

She walked into the kitchen area and opened the refrigerator. She noted that the handles were also gold.

Inside were fruit platters. Meat and cheese trays. It was as if appetizers for an upcoming party had been prepared. And she took them all out, happily examining them.

"These will do nicely."

She put them on the countertop and uncovered them, scrounging until she found a plate and filling it with a generous portion from each tray. Then she hunted around until she found sparkling water and poured herself a glass.

And all the while he watched her, leaning back against the island, his palms pressed down into the surface, his forearms flexed.

"I have staff for that," he said.

"Well, I was able to dish myself an entire plate without you summoning anyone, so I think it all worked out in the end."

She looked around and saw that there was no dining table in the space. So she took it all to the low, leather couch that faced floor-to-ceiling windows that overlooked the city. She sat down and popped a grape into her mouth. "This is quite nice."

"Thank you," he said, dryly.

"I always try to be polite."

"What game are you playing?"

"I'm not playing a game. I feel that you are a game player, and therefore cannot figure out what I'm doing. And what confuses you most is that I'm not doing anything. I'm not. I am not doing anything, and I do not wish to be doing anything, and I am no threat to you at all. I am simply me. I have changed. I was only ever the Eloise that you knew because of my mother. And I have worked very hard to become the Eloise that I am. Stop looking for the snake in the grass. It isn't me."

"How do I…"

"You came to me, Vincenzo. If you had not, I would never have come back here."

"You acquiesced easily."

"Yes. Because I meant what I said. If you need help, I wish to help you. You are trying to rescue your country, at least, as far as I can tell, reading between the lines of your grim threats. I respect that. Your father has done a terrible job with this country, and it sounds to me as if you are the only person willing to do something to save it. And the fact that you are willing to turn the power over to the people… For all your bluster I do believe that you are well-meaning. I do believe that you want to do the right thing by your country. The palace staff were always kind to me. Regardless of the drama happening between your parents and my mother. They were always so very kind. I feel… Even though it was isolated, Arista has been my home for as long as anywhere else. It matters to me what you're doing. So I'll help. But I don't want to enrich myself or anything like that." She ate a piece of cheese. "Though, I'm not averse to enjoying some nice food."

And for his part, he was actually stunned into silence, which was really quite something.

But it wasn't long after that her clothing arrived. And she was whisked off to change yet again. Wrapped in that brilliant green gown that was now custom fitted to her curves.

And when they exited the hotel, the press was there. Flashbulbs went off, the melee surrounding them intense.

"Is that Eloise St. George? Your father's mistress? Where has she been hiding?" The press volleyed questions, a pounding insistent drum, and it took her back.

All the way to when she'd been eighteen and heartbroken, tender in her feelings for Vincenzo still and somehow being cast as a whore in a play with his father on the world stage.

Her heart was pounding so hard she thought she might vomit.

"Yes, it is Eloise St. George," he answered. "And

you know the old stories about her. But you do not know the truth of how she came to be at the palace. Her mother has lived as my father's mistress since Eloise was six. Eloise and I have known each other since childhood. I, like many of you, blamed her for my father's behavior at the time. She was eighteen. My father was a king. I am not blameless, but the press hounded her, treated her as the villain in the piece. We are here to unmask the real villain."

"Your father's mistress?" one of the men asked. "It was reported that the indiscretion with Eloise St George was the only…"

"You will find that my father is economical with the truth as it suits. That the King has not held himself to the same standards that he holds his people. You may be quite shocked to learn just how deeply my father has let down Arista."

"Do you have proof?" another reporter asked.

"I have lots of proof," he said. "I will happily give it to you. But now I must take Eloise to dine at the palace. It has been a long time coming for her. I am here to tell my father that he is ruined."

He grinned then, the smile of a predator that made her shiver down to her bones. "And believe me when I tell you, you will have all the information you need to ensure the ruination is complete."

# CHAPTER FIVE

HE ALMOST FELT sorry for Eloise. Almost. She was pale and drawn and quiet as the limousine inched ever closer to the palace.

She had been nearly silent ever since the reporters had ambushed them outside his penthouse. And it had only become more pronounced with each passing moment since. He could feel her dread, feel it radiating off her.

"You are nervous?" he asked.

For the first time he felt… He had miscalculated. She was hurt by all of this. More distressed than he'd assumed. He had thought her hard. He had made assumptions about who and what she was based on his belief in her guilt when it came to her relationship with his father.

And he'd let that form his image of her all these years. Anything to replace the one he'd had back when they'd been young.

They arrived at the palace, and he felt his own stomach tense. He felt her entire body go rigid.

He had not been back here since his mother had died. And it had been her death a year ago that had triggered this plan.

He'd come only to say goodbye to her, and he could still remember the stale feeling in the room. All the bitterness from so many years steeped in it.

It lingered. In the air. In him.

They got out of the car at the front entrance, the grand double doors opening slowly. The palace was a gleaming white, a testament to the unending purity of its ruler. The spires were gold. It was not an accident that in his own building he employed the use of concrete and gold. An echo of what his father was, and the lack of pretense with which Vincenzo presented himself.

Symbolism that no one would ever appreciate except for him, he had a feeling. And yet, appreciate it he did.

He took her arm, and the two of them stood at the threshold to the palace, and suddenly she began to... Laugh.

"What?"

"Oh, I just... This would've been my dream. When I was sixteen years old. Arriving at the palace with you. I would've felt... I would have felt like the luckiest girl in the world."

"Well, you are quite undermining my presence, at the moment. As it is intended to be a bit more ominous. Giggling is hardly the tone we want to set."

"What you're sharing with the world is ominous enough. We have to belabor it by acting like a funeral procession?"

"Did you want it to be a family reunion?"

"Hardly." She made a strange, strangled sound. "We are practically stepsiblings."

He nearly recoiled. "We are nothing of the kind. Our parents are not married."

They stopped and looked at each other for a beat. And he felt a burn start in his blood. But it wasn't just that. It was an unexpected solidarity.

He had thought to force her here, but she had offered to come.

As a friend.

Even after everything, she had offered that.

They were announced and led through the grand corridors of the palace, on through to the great dining hall, where his father was seated at the head of the table and there, at his right-hand side was Eloise's mother.

She looked up, her eyes like glittering bright jewels. Her fingernails were long, red claws.

She had not been permitted to sit in that position when his mother had still been living. And he could see that she took a great joy in flaunting this change in his face.

"How wonderful that you could join us this evening," she said, acting the part of hostess.

It made his stomach curdle.

"Of course."

"The other guests will arrive shortly," his father said.

And it took a moment. Just a moment. For Eloise's mother to recognize her. And a moment longer for his father to do the same.

"What is this?" his father asked.

"Oh," he said. "Eloise is here. As my mistress. I find that I have taken a great liking to her of late."

Her mother looked at her daughter with a dismissive sneer.

"That is impossible," she said. "She has gained at least two stone since she was here last. I should think that a man of your pedigree would have better taste."

What surprised him, as much as the moment of camaraderie he'd felt with her outside, was the rage he felt toward her mother just then. Had he not himself been hard on her when he'd first encountered her again? He knew he had been. But it was not this.

The way she looked at Eloise...

She hated her, he realized. Because she was young and beautiful, whatever the woman said. Her own daughter outshone her and she couldn't stand it.

"Oh, my taste is impeccable," he said. "And I find each and every curve of her body to my liking. More than that, I have decided to go public with it. And with our relationship."

"All the guests here tonight are well aware of the

nature of my relationship with Cressida St. George. It is my inner circle."

"I'm sure, Father," he said. "But your cronies are one thing—the public is quite another. I have already spoken with the press. Of course, they all remember the one sin you were ever caught in. But you made sure to assassinate her character. To make it seem as if you were only a victim. But I have evidence to the contrary, and I will make sure the world knows. Not only of your sexual indiscretion but of all you have stolen from Arista. You have defrauded this land, and its people, and I intend to see your wrongs exposed, and made right."

His father began to turn a particular shade of purple, but it was then that the other dignitaries and diplomats began to line the table.

Eloise, for her part, looked subdued. Then as he made conversation with the men around him, making provocative statements about the economy of Arista, he felt her shrinking beside him.

And again the urge to protect her was strong. He could not explain it; he was here on a mission that concerned his country, his revenge. And yet he felt consumed by her. And that had not been part of the plan.

Tonight, he decided he would say no more to his father. Tonight, he made it his mission to speak only to the other men present. And he also left the table at the precise moment all of the other guests did. His father tried to catch him.

"Eloise and I are returning to my flat," he said. "I rather would like an early night with her. Surely that's something you can understand."

"You were raised with her," he said.

"And you took advantage of her," Vincenzo said. "Which I will not do. But you did that often, didn't you?"

"You will not make these things public," his father said.

"I already have."

But then his father reached out and grabbed Eloise by the arm. "If you wish to play the whore…"

"I never did," she said. "And you know it. But you let the story go out as it did because you thought it such a great distraction to the reality of what you were doing. I understand that now. That my image, my body, was something you could trade on. A way to try and play the victim. Someone got too close to the truth, but they were just wrong enough that being handed me as a scandal kept them from my mother."

Vincenzo only stood, frozen. There were few times in his life when he had felt that he might be outside his understanding. Once had been when Eloise had kissed him, and he'd sent her away in spite of a roaring need to drive himself inside her.

And now.

He'd had no idea. He never had.

"I didn't know why I came back," she said, her voice sounding strangely detached now. "But I realize now. It was to have a front seat at your deposition. You destroyed me for all the world to see, but I refused to let that be the last word. It will be mine. The last word will be mine. You could not force me to be your mistress, you could not shame me into vanishing and you will not cow me into silence. You are a twisted, perverse old man, and you may have made my mother your puppet, but you never succeeded in making me anything. Neither did you, Mother," she said, looking her mother in the eye. "All that I am, I am because of myself."

She turned then, walking out of the ballroom. He stood for a moment and realized that his place was with her for now. For had he not brought her here? Was her distress, her pain not his fault?

He had believed a lie for years. He had been his father's pawn much the same as anyone else, and it galled as much as the guilt that now assaulted him.

"Eloise," he said, following her. "Tell me."

"Now you want to know? You should have always known, Vincenzo. You of all people should have always known."

"How?" he asked, and yet he felt his failure like a howling beast inside his lungs.

"You knew me."

"I thought I did. But then you kissed me."

"And that made me a whore?"

"No," he said. "You said you loved me. I thought anyone who loved me… I could not believe it. I could much more easily believe you were using me all along."

In those words was a sadness he never wanted to examine.

"I was never using you," she said, unshed tears in her eyes.

"Eloise…"

"After all of that I just wanted to start over. I never wanted to be here again. I never wanted any of this. I thought… I thought I could just put it behind me."

"But you came with me. When I asked. You came with me."

Her eyes glittered. "Yes. I did. I thought I was fine. I thought therapy fixed all of this but… I'm angry. I am angry. My mother made me hate my body—your father made me afraid of it."

And for the first time, true sympathy curled inside him. Not just the first time he had ever felt sympathy for her. Possibly the first time he had ever felt sympathy for anyone.

And he felt a black sort of blinding rage at his father that was different than the rage he had carried around inside him all this time. It was different.

They went back to the penthouse, and when they walked inside, he looked at her silhouette against the city lights below.

"Are you all right to continue?"

"I knew the history between myself and your father. Even if you did not."

"He did not ever..."

"No. But I fear that he would have."

"You're very brave, Eloise," he said, the compliment foreign on his lips.

She turned and looked over her shoulder, smiling. Her blond hair cascaded down her back in golden waves, and he had the urge to touch it, but also... In the wake of what she had told him, he felt he ought not to.

"Thank you," she said. "I do not feel brave sometimes. Rather I have chosen to hide myself away, and there are times when I question that. But I am happy. I am content. Is there more to life than that?"

"I am not happy or content," he said. "So I suppose we can debate whether or not there is more than that."

"Indeed." She looked at him for a long moment. "I wanted you," she said. "Please know that. It was not simply manipulation or loneliness. I know that I was too young. But what I felt for you was genuine. That means something to me."

Then she turned and walked into her bedroom, leaving him standing there feeling speechless. And there was nothing half so remarkable as that.

# CHAPTER SIX

WELL, SHE HAD done it. She had confronted the King. She had spoken the truth.

She knew the King's behavior wasn't her fault. She knew that it was the kind of man the King was. It had nothing to do with the kind of woman she was. Nothing to do with anything she put off, nothing to do with the shape of her body. There was nothing wrong with her.

But she still felt shame, especially when the King had looked at her last night, and she hated that.

What a strange thing to be back. To be confronted with all these things that she had been convinced she had dealt with on some level. She supposed that she had. She wasn't reduced to a crying mess or anything like that. It was just that she felt… It was just that she felt. And tonight they were to return to the palace for a ball celebrating the five hundredth year of the Moretti Rule.

It was tonight, she knew, that Vincenzo would ensure it all burned.

She knew that because it would be poetic to him. Of that she was certain. This claim that he was going to disrupt the line, he would do it on the anniversary of his family's rule, because he liked the symmetry of it. Because he would like the poetic bent to the justice.

She wasn't sure justice sounded anything like poetry to her.

But it appeased some dark piece of her heart she'd thought long dealt with.

Who didn't want to stand before their abusers and tell them what they thought?

When the news had broken of her supposed relationship with the King she'd been devastated. And she'd lost the one ally she'd thought she had.

Vincenzo.

She had to wonder if, in the end, it was Vincenzo who had hurt her worst of all.

Because she'd never believed in her mother, or his father for that matter.

But she'd believed in him.

She shook off those thoughts and decided on a walk. She went down through the marketplace, away from the center of the city, and found a farmers market. She bought flowers. So many flowers. Enough that her arms were completely full by the time she left. Then she went up to the penthouse—her thumbprint granting her access for the time she was staying there—and began to place flowers in vases on every available surface.

When Vincenzo appeared, he was shirtless. There was sweat rolling down his chest, and his cheekbones were highlighted by slashes of red. "What the hell is this?"

"Oh," she said. "I thought you were... In bed."

"I've been out for a run," he said. "What is this?"

"I thought that some flowers would brighten the place. I love flowers."

He blinked. "I have never had flowers in here."

"You also don't really have any color. This is much nicer, don't you think?"

He shook his head. "I do not think."

"Do not be a beast, Vincenzo," she said, continuing to arrange the flowers.

He took a deep breath and crossed his arms. "I've been thinking about my father," Vincenzo said.

"Yes?"

"He is a bastard."

"No argument from me."

"If you do not wish to participate in this..."

Her fingers stilled, her eyes lifting to his. "Are you asking what I want?"

His expression was grim. "Yes."

Her heart felt tender. She could leave. She could go right now. Forget this was happening in Arista. He could complete his vengeance without her.

"Vincenzo, do you believe me now?"

"Yes," he said, his voice tight. "I am…sorry."

"Have you ever told anyone you're sorry before?"

He looked away. "I have never been sorry before. I am now."

She thought her chest might crack. "I accept your apology."

"Would you like to leave?"

"No," she said. "I might be having difficulty sorting through my feelings on the matter. And I am not entirely certain that I'm… Happy. Or enjoying this, but I do think it needs to be done. And in some ways I think it is good that I'm bearing witness to it. But in the meantime, I would like to collect flowers, and do things to make myself feel more comfortable."

"Of course."

"There is the matter of the gold dress…"

It was so revealing. And she had felt sick over that when he had first put her in it. For a variety of reasons. But now…

She did not want to act out of a sense of fear. Or a sense of shame. She wanted to be… Well, if he thought she was beautiful, then she wanted to be that kind of beautiful. For her. For him.

Maybe she shouldn't want to be beautiful for him. But she did.

Because it was a tender bloom in the center of her, of a girlish fantasy that had been as breathless as it was innocent. Something that she had lost later.

Something that had been tainted thereafter. "You are worried about it?"

She was, but she...decided to let it go. "Really, the thing that I'm most worried about is having to dance."

"We do have to dance," he said.

"I figured as much. But we are making a statement, are we not?" She imitated his tone and arched a brow in what she hoped was a decent impression of his arrogant expressions. "We must make a show."

"Are you mocking me?"

"If you have to ask, I'm not doing a very good job."

"No one dares to mock me."

"I dare. And quite handily too. I am sorry if it disagrees with your royal constitution."

"I'm glad to see you are not quite so timid as you were last night."

"I was not timid in the end."

"No," he said, smiling. "You were not."

It was his smile that undid her.

"Shall we practice dancing?"

"No," he said.

"Please?"

"You wish to practice now?"

He gestured to his bare chest, and she could not help but take a visual tour of his body. Glistening and tan, with just the right amount of dark hair sprinkled over his muscles. His pectorals, his abs. She wanted to touch him. And the inclination she felt toward him was quite a bit different than the one she had felt when she was eighteen. For she had imagined gauzy things. Sweet kisses and touches, and him laying her down on the soft mattress. Here she could easily imagine his hot skin. Sweat slicked. She knew his mouth would be firm, and that his whiskers would scratch her face. She could picture him putting his hand between her legs and…

She bit her lip.

Her fantasies had certainly progressed, even if her experience had not.

But she could imagine—vividly—what she wanted from him. She wanted to inhale all that testosterone. She could remember vaguely being concerned about his chest hair back when she had been eighteen. In fact, she had been afraid that she would not like to touch it, which was a problem, as she did want him, she had told herself.

Now she wished to run her hands over his body, chest hair and all. She wanted to lick him. Even sweaty. Maybe most especially sweaty.

The desire was deep, and it was visceral. And she was not ashamed. She wasn't ashamed.

She was a woman. And he was a man. An attractive man, and she wanted him.

Her body was her own. But he could borrow it. And he could use it. She would greatly enjoy that.

"If you wish," she said.

And he took two steps toward her, his dark eyes blazing, and she realized then that he was certain he was calling her bluff. Instead, she took a step toward him and held out her hand. "Let us dance."

He pulled her up against him, and she could feel that his chest was damp through the fabric of her top. He was hard. And just as hot as she had imagined. She put her hand on his bare shoulder, could feel the play of his muscles beneath her fingertips. And he grasped her hand in his. "I have made it no secret that I think you're beautiful."

"It is only our connection that prevents you from finding me… How did you put it? Beddable?"

She was being more bold, more forward than she had ever intended to be.

And she felt… Giddy with it. Not ashamed. Not worried.

"Yes. I believe I did."

A great many words bottled up in her throat. He thought her a victim now, or something close to it. Did that mean he no longer found her beddable? Or did it mean he found her more so because he found her innocent in that way?

She didn't know. And she supposed the only way to find out would be to make an actual move on him. But she stopped herself just short of that.

And instead, tried to focus on what it felt like to be held in his arms. To follow the steady rhythm of the dance. Even though there was no music.

And the absurdity of it all would've made her laugh if she could breathe. But she couldn't.

"You're a very good dancer," she said, her eyes focused on his chest. The golden skin there. The muscle definition. The hair…

"Hazard of my upbringing."

"I didn't learn to dance."

"You seem perfectly competent at it."

"Oh, I am. I used to watch. I used to watch from upstairs. When your family would have balls."

"Your mother went."

"Yes," she said. "But there was… My mother enjoyed the attention. The drama. In a way that I never could. Anyway, it was thought that I would draw attention. The kind they didn't want. The kind they didn't like."

"I've never been able to figure out exactly what manner of sadist my father is. The way that he hurt my mother. And the way that he… The way that he treated yours."

"I think you'll find my mother quite likes being involved in the pain, whether she's dishing it out or taking it."

"That may be. But there is an element to it that I… I can't absolve him of. Not anymore. After knowing what he did to you."

"My mother knew. She is still with him. Do not absolve her simply because you are refocusing your anger. No, your father isn't a good man. There is no disputing that, but my mother is not a victim."

"Perhaps it is possible to be both. The predator and the prey."

She frowned. She wanted only to focus on him. On his body, on his beauty. She wanted to focus on the warmth of his body, the strength of his hold. The fantasy inherent in this moment, and not the reality of their lives. Never that.

One thing was certain—they had both suffered for the games their parents played. Whoever's door had most of the blame heaped at it.

"It will be fascinating," she said. "To be down in the ballroom tonight."

"Yes. No longer the secret."

Recognition bloomed in her chest. "I think I must want that."

"What?"

"I am marveling at my own motives," she said. "I cannot say that I have figured them out entirely. I have lived a quiet life these last few years, and I said that I would never return here. That I would never… That I would never see you again. And that I was happy for it."

"I see."

"Yet here I am. Dancing with you. Here I am, leaping headfirst into this retribution."

"Perhaps you are just as filled with hate as I am."

She smiled up at him, but she felt the expression

falter as her eyes collided with his. "But that can't be. Because I have worked very hard and I..."

"All that therapy," he said. "You think you should be more enlightened than I am?"

"I know I should be," she said.

"Reality is often a difficult thing. What we might like is not always what is. Aren't our entire lives a testament to that? Isn't all that we've been through a testament to that?"

"Maybe that's why I prefer the fantasy. Of gardens and a quiet life. A little stone house."

"I can see how it might appeal," he said.

She looked up at him again, and she felt something electric when their eyes clashed.

"You can?"

"For a moment. Like smelling the scent of roses on the breeze. And it catches you, for a breath. And then it's gone and you're left to wonder if it was there at all. I can sense it that way. I can feel it that way. The impression of a life lived quietly. Of a life lived only for yourself."

"I hadn't thought of it that way." But he was not wrong. She had removed every responsibility she might feel toward another person. Every hint of caring about outside expectations. She had sunk deeply into her own reality. Only her. Only her flowers. Only the things that made her happy and none of the things that didn't. And so she had been unprepared. Her emotions still in that same deep freeze when he had come to see her. She had been unprepared for what it would do to her. Unprepared for what being back in Arista would mean. Or maybe *unprepared* was the wrong word. Blissfully, intentionally disconnected from it.

But now she was here. And she felt anger. For the girl she had been. And a heady rush of need for the man that he was.

He felt like the reward she had been hoping for all this time. The reward that she deserved after living a life so disconnected. After being denied so many things when she was a girl.

And without thought, she moved her hand from his shoulder and slid it down the front of his chest. Pressed over where his heartbeat was, and she felt it raging. She looked up at him, her heart pounding an intense tattoo in time.

"Vincenzo…"

"That is enough," he said, moving away from her. "Tonight is the night that I tell my father no matter what. No matter how he tries to clean up after this, it is no use. I am his heir, and I refuse to carry the line forward. And he will have to face that."

"I admire your rage," she said.

"Why is that?"

She felt separation between them like she had been stabbed. "Because it's clean. And bright. Because it is…real. It is that which I admire most. The honesty in it."

* * *

"You seem quite honest, Eloise."

"I try to be. But then I wonder. If I have been the least bit honest with myself. I didn't think I was angry anymore. I thought I'd put it all away. What does it mean that I haven't?"

He stopped, his hand lifting, hovering over her cheek, as if he wished to touch her. To maybe offer comfort?

"You are human," he said, lowering his hand.

She ignored her disappointment. "Is that what you are? Human?"

"I cannot afford to be human. I must be the cleanup crew. I must fix all that he has broken. And I cannot allow myself to be distracted."

He strode from the room, leaving her standing there. Her hand burned where she had touched him, and her heart... Her heart burned too. Her heart burned with an intensity that she could not identify.

She felt like she was on the edges of her own life. The pull to Virginia was strong, but she wasn't there. She was here. And she felt like... Something was going to break.

She was afraid that it was going to be her.

# CHAPTER SEVEN

WHEN ELOISE EMERGED, ready for the ball, his gut tightened with the need that defied everything else. He'd had to walk away from her earlier. The touch of her delicate fingertips against his skin almost more than he could bear. He did not wish to be so attracted to her.

What he'd said to her when she was eighteen was just as true now. She was bound to him in ways she had not chosen. They were bound to one another in this sadistic farce.

He was a man who owned his appetites. But he was also a man who protected those weaker than himself. A man who did not believe in using his power against others. Eloise had chosen to be here, but he had to wonder how much of the past's sins had dictated that.

His father had hurt her unforgivably—he could see that now.

And it shamed him, tenfold.

Because even if she had slept with him, that would have been true.

He had somehow realized she was young and a victim of circumstance when she had kissed him. When she had come to his room.

And he had forgotten it all when he'd been hurt by her. Had recast her as the villain the moment he'd found it convenient.

It shamed him.

But now Eloise was standing before him wearing that revealing gold dress and looking like a goddess reborn. Like she had just emerged from fire, a glorious avenging sexuality that he wanted to hold against his body. She was glorious. When he could think of nothing more poetic than his father having to witness her being part of his downfall. She was a fresh-faced glory, her cheeks pink and tinged with something gold like the dress, her lips a glossy rose with an underlying flame.

And he could not help himself. He wanted her.

But it was not Eloise who was unworthy.

It was him.

One thing was for sure, she might've had therapy. She might arrive in a place that she considered healthy, but healthy was the furthest thing from his mind. Because his life was not divorced of responsibility. Because he could not go off and live that quiet life that called to him like a rose petal on the wind. He could not. Because he had to save Arista. Because he had to make sure his father's legacy wasn't immortalized in glowing terms and song, but that he was remembered as he'd truly been.

He must.

And so if all the things inside him remained twisted, it was because they were twisted around these inevitabilities.

He could not be another man, and he would not seek to try. He would not turn away from all that he must do.

But he did not wish to turn away from the beauty that was before him either.

Whatever he might deserve.

He held his hand out, and she took it. A tentative light in her eyes.

And he wanted to banish that tentativeness. He wanted to tell her definitively that he would defend her. That he would slay every dragon.

Because he was piecing together these things, these events that had occurred. From the first time he had seen her when she was six years old to that time she had gone to his room and confessed her love to him in what he thought to be a brazen sort of manipulation. But if he saw it differently. If he looked at her differently, if he banished that cynicism that was so forceful inside of him...

Maybe she had loved him.

Maybe when she'd come to his room, when she'd

kissed him, it had been with more sincerity and heart than he'd ever had inside his body.

A gift he had not known how to receive.

It made his chest feel like fire.

She had gone away and hidden, protected herself in the wake of his betrayal, because he could see that clearly now.

He had been the one who had wronged her.

Enormously.

He was not a man who understood love, but loyalty at least, he had made it a point to know. Honor. He had not acted with honor. She had been his friend, all because she had reached out to him. All because of her spirit, which was lovelier than his would ever be.

He had accused her of whoring herself out. He had paid her to leave.

She had gone away and made a quiet life for herself. And she was correct. He was the one who had sought her out. So if he removed all of his presuppositions and the deep, entrenched and unfair thoughts that he had been directing at her for all these years... He was left with the woman standing before him. Strong when those around her who should've protected her had not been. Filled with honor and integrity. With strength. A girl who had thrived in spite of the lack of care.

A wildflower left to grow on her own in the garden, who had fought her way through, without being consumed by weeds.

She was that wild garden at the house in Virginia that he had thought was unkempt. It was not.

For it tended itself, and it thrived in the wild.

Just as Eloise did.

They should all be so lucky as to have that kind of strength inside of them.

He himself? He was oriented to vengeance. But she had seen to her healing.

There was a power in her choice that he had never known before. That he had never seen.

They got in the limousine and were silent on the drive to the palace this time. His own thoughts were turning. He was ready for this. More than ready.

But he had not anticipated that so much of his thought would be with her. How could he have? For his entire opinion on her had changed in just a couple of days.

The palace was open, brightly lit and glittering. Lights were strong over the courtyards, with guests spilling outside.

One of his father's perfectly immaculate glittering affairs.

These were not the sorts of debauched parties he had in secret. No. These were demonstrations of wealth and goodness, and only if you knew, only if you really knew, could you sense that hint of disreputability beneath it all.

But it was there.

And he knew it well.

The truth of the fact was that his father was often sleeping with his friends' wives. That there were no fences built by marriage vows, none that could not be handily crushed by the cavalier nature of the way all of these people treated relationships. But that was only what you would see if you wished to dig beneath the surface.

And none of the casual guests would. They would all simply enjoy the opulence around them and not dig at all into the glittering, terrible underbelly.

But, as he and Eloise walked into the ballroom, a hush came over the room, and he knew that his statements from yesterday had done their job. They had been in the media. And everyone here had heard the rumors, and here he was, and here she was. A bright beacon of truth. Substantiating those claims.

Here they were together. A reckoning.

"They know," he said. "And tonight, they have all turned up to see what will happen."

"It is amazing your father hasn't disbarred you from the event," she said.

"He won't. He won't because he knows that doing so will only create more rumor. And at this point, the scandal is already out of his control. He will not wish to be pressed."

"And you will press him," she said.

"Without hesitation," he responded. "But first, a dance."

He led her out to the middle of the dance floor and pressed her luscious body against his. For a moment, he forgot where they were. For a moment, he forgot why they were here. Every eye in the room was on them. Every eye filled with curiosity, but he did not care. For what he wanted, what he really wanted was to have Eloise in his arms. Her soft skin beneath his hands.

She had become a symbol of his retribution. She had become a symbol of all of this. While she most of all was suddenly what he now wanted to avenge. More even than his mother.

As he looked at her angelic face, he could not explain why it had become suddenly the driving force, the driving need.

But it had.

She was the most important thing. She was everything.

Eloise.

The desire for her was like a fire in his blood, and for a moment, that thought gave him pause. Because he wondered if this heat in his blood was anything like his father's.

Vincenzo had never wanted a woman. Not a specific woman.

He desired women. He liked them in all their

shapes and forms. But... He had never been sick with his desire for a specific one.

And here he was.

He wanted her above all else. He wanted her more than revenge. He wanted her more than his next breath.

He traced his finger along the line of her jaw, and he felt her shiver beneath his touch.

He lowered his head, a breath away. "You are beautiful," he said.

"I feel beautiful."

Not foolish. For she had said so many times that she feared feeling foolish. But she did not feel as if her body was the sort that would create the reaction that he anticipated, but he could not see what she saw. He could only see desirability. He could only see beauty. But he could also see that it mattered what she thought of her own self. What she thought of her body. And he cared about that.

Another foreign feeling. Caring about another person in this way.

He had cared only about justice for a very long time.

Now he found he cared about her feelings.

And that was a novelty.

But he could not call it anything half so light as a novelty, not with any honesty. It was a pain that started at the center of his chest and burned outward like a wildfire. He looked over her shoulder and saw his father. Watching.

Even the King was watching.

Good.

He hoped that he was anticipating what came next.

The gaze of his father made him refocus. On his revenge. And that was when he decided to lean in and taste her lips. He felt her breath draw in just as his mouth touched hers. And he tasted that sweetness.

That rose petal on the wind. That glorious hint that filled his lungs if only for a moment before vanishing. Like a bright white moment of clarity. Of possibility. And suddenly, with that soft mouth beneath his own, everything seemed possible. They seemed possible.

And when they parted, it was gone. A hint of a memory that might've been a dream, because all that remained was Vincenzo. And all that he had yet to do.

"It is time," he said.

He moved away from her and made his way over to his father. "Congratulations," he said. "On the long-standing lineage of the Moretti family. Is that not why we are all here to celebrate?"

"It is why I could not bar you from the festivities. Yes."

"A tragedy for you," he said, feeling his mouth curve into a cruel smile even as he spoke. "But I think what I have to say about the Moretti family is something that all the guests in attendance may wish to hear."

He turned and, with an effortless ease, projected his voice over the din of the crowd. And he did not sound like an unhinged voice in the street, rather he spoke with the confidence and authority that flowed through his veins. "The Moretti family bloodline is filled with poison," he said. "There is no one who knows this better than Eloise St. George and myself. We have joined together, united as one in this common belief. The Moretti line must end. And it must be exposed for what it is. You, who have sat here in riches while your people starved. Who have rained the judgment down upon them while you engaged in every kind of debauchery. While you kept a mistress for more than twenty years in the same home as your wife, flaunting her as an assistant, using state funds to support the lifestyle. And then attempting to manipulate her daughter into an affair with you, and allowing the media to crucify her when she refused you. Using your power and position and lording it over the women around you. You are a man with no honor. You are a man with no dignity. You are no kind of man. And I will take over the throne, and when I do I will begin to dismantle the line. Your precious bloodline. As destroyed as your reputation will be, once the truth I have about you is disseminated in the media."

"Whatever it is you're doing," his father said. "It

will not work. The country needs me. The country needs the monarchy."

"The country needs nothing of the kind. I have been building the infrastructure right beneath your nose. Establishing the scaffolding required for everything to go on when you are no longer at the helm." His blood burned with anger, but this was different. This was a righteous, unending anger that flowed through him. And it did not feel toxic or calcified.

It was alive and so was he.

"Oh, yes. I have been pouring money into this nation for years. Under the guise of being an anonymous benefactor, foreign aid. Foreign aid you should be ashamed to accept given the amount of money that flows through your coffers. But you are not. Because you are greedy. Because you are corrupt. And when I ascend the throne, it will be to dismantle everything that you have built. The machine that you have created. And having me killed will solve nothing. Nothing at all. For even then you will lose your bloodline. I am not your ally, old man. And I have never been. And the line will die with me. For I will never have an heir. And the government will be turned over to the people. The Moretti line will not prevail for another five hundred years. It will not even prevail past the end of my life. I will deny you that. You will not live to see it, but you will live knowing it. You will watch the foundation of all that you are crumble. The rewriting of what will be in the history books after you are gone."

The room around them might have been a hundred yards in the distance, for in this moment, there was only him. Only his father.

"No one cares about a few women," his father sneered.

"Perhaps. Many do not. A small sin in this world. But it is not your only sin. And the rest? Do you think it was only my mother's life that spared you my wrath? I cared about her, but if I'd had all the evidence I needed to make sure your reign ended, unequivocally, when I revealed you, I would have done so on any given Tuesday. I don't require theatrics."

His father looked truly afraid now, and Vincenzo relished it. "I don't mind them, though." He grinned, and he knew it was filled with all the hatred that insulated his heart. "I have everything now. It is all in order. I was finally able to pay off one of your most trusted accountants to get me absolute proof of how you siphon money away from the people, and there may be those who will turn a blind eye to your sexual exploits, but what you have done to Arista? The name of Moretti will cease to exist. And what was it all for?"

He took a step closer to his father, and he felt as if someone had grabbed hold of his heart and taken it in their hand. Was holding it in place. Keeping it from beating. For he saw… Not the raging monster of his mind. But a man coming to the end of his years.

A man who was only a man.

"You are nothing but an old man who has left a legacy of pain. That is what you will leave in this world. It will be fixed when you are gone, and no one will think of you. You will die, and that will be the end of you."

"You would not dare. You would not dare do this. It does not benefit you."

"I don't care about power," Vincenzo said. "It is of no consequence to me."

"You… You think you're better than me. And here you are parading in with the same sort of whore that I have favored these many years. She would've warmed my bed if she had stayed longer. They all do in the end."

"That's a lie," Eloise said, her voice cutting over the sound of the gasps in the room. "I would never have warmed your bed. I denied you. When you came for me when I was only eighteen years old. I denied you."

His father's face contorted then, into an ugly, hateful sneer, and Vincenzo felt as if they were all watching him unmask himself. "You can say whatever you like, but the newspapers already spoke their piece. And people will always wonder."

"But I won't," she said. "And I am not hungry for a certain kind of reputation. I am only hungry for freedom. And I can have that. I will have it. You are nothing but a bitter, sad old man. Twisted. If you did not have power and money, no woman would touch you. And that is the difference between you and Vincenzo."

Vincenzo felt as if he'd been shot. Her defense of him, after all he had done.

"He does not crave it because he does not need it," she continued, all her righteous fire spilling from her, filling the room. "You do. You need to have power over the people that you manipulate into your sphere. Over the women that you manipulate into your bed. They must be afraid of you. You would've forced me, and we both know it. Even though the rumors leaked to the press were wrong, they were what rescued me. Because it was the rumors that made Vincenzo give me the money to leave. And I am grateful for that every day. Had I not been rescued by default of being sent away, I know that you would've forced me into your bed. You would've made me into another of your secrets. And I know what it's like to live my life as a secret. But I will not. Not anymore. Hiding was easier, because it allowed me to make my life mine. But I will not be cowed. Not for any reason. Not for anything. I am not afraid of you. I am not a powerless girl. And no one should be afraid of you. Everyone should know what you are, openly. So that no one is keeping your secrets, and no one is trying to pretend."

"You bitch of a girl," he said.

"That is enough," Vincenzo said, stepping forward. "Eloise is a woman. Filled with bravery and integrity, and she makes the world better for being in it. Something you will never ever understand. You are nothing but a coward. Your entire kingdom is built upon perfidy. It is built upon lies. And tonight it is finished. In the future it will be finished for good."

"You are dead to me," his father said.

Vincenzo turned. "I would love to say that you were dead to me. But you are not. You are very much alive. And until you are dead, you will not be able to be dead to me. Because I must fight against you. You have made it so. I refuse to allow you to exist as you do. To be as you are. What I want you to know is that you are a fool. Believing that I was simply distant. Believing that I was not secretly acting against you all this time. You are a man of great manipulation. But it did not occur to you that your own son might have secrets of his own. Did not occur to you that your own son might be hiding the truth of the matter from you. And of course it never occurred to you that you might miss something."

"You cannot do this."

"I have. The ball is in motion. All the information that I've compiled about you is being sent out to various news sources automatically tonight. And I daresay there will be a reckoning about what took place in this very ballroom. I cannot imagine that all your guests will remain tight-lipped. Many of them will be rushing to speak against you. To make it clear that they do not wish to associate with you in any way. They will all flee from you like rats from a sinking ship. Even your mistress would be wise to do the same."

"You cannot…"

"I have done my part," Vincenzo said. "The rest will unfold on its own. It is over now. You do not deserve silence. And no one here deserves protection. I would remember that when you all go out into the world. You must choose a side. I would advise you choose the side that stands against him."

He looked over at Eloise, who was burning bright, her breath coming in harsh, sharp bursts. Eloise. She would not be broken by this. Because she was not the fragile wisp of a creature he had deemed her when she'd come to his bed and kissed him. She was not the great manipulator he had allowed himself to believe she was thereafter.

She was strong. And she was brilliant.

And he was trying to think now of all that he could give her.

*Make her your mistress.*

No. It was impossible. That was the only thing that burned now. She could not be his mistress, because he would not dishonor her in that way. And he would not take a wife.

But she could be his. For the night.

# Loyal Readers
# FREE BOOKS Voucher

## We're giving away **THOUSANDS** of **FREE BOOKS**

# Get up to 4
# FREE FABULOUS BOOKS
## You Love!

To thank you for being a loyal reader we'd like to send you up to 4 FREE BOOKS, absolutely free.

Just write "YES" on the Loyal Reader Voucher and we'll send you up to 4 Free Books and Free Mystery Gifts, altogether worth over $20, as a way of saying thank you for being a loyal reader.

Try **Harlequin® Desire** books featuring the worlds of the American elite with juicy plot twists, delicious sensuality and intriguing scandal.

Try **Harlequin Presents®** Larger-print books featuring the glamourous lives of royals and billionaires in a world of exotic locations, where passion knows no bounds.

Or **TRY BOTH!**

We are so glad you love the books as much as we do and can't wait to send you great new books.

So don't miss out, return your Loyal Reader Voucher Today!

*Pam Powers*

# LOYAL READER
# FREE BOOKS VOUCHER

**YES! I Love Reading, please send me up to 4 FREE BOOKS and Free Mystery Gifts from the series I select.**

Just write in "YES" on the dotted line below then return this card today and we'll send your free books & gifts asap!

➡ ~~YES~~ ⬅

Which do you prefer?

☐ **Harlequin Desire®**
225/326 HDL GRGA

☐ **Harlequin Presents® Larger Print**
176/376 HDL GRGA

☐ **BOTH**
225/326 & 176/376
HDL GRGM

FIRST NAME | LAST NAME

ADDRESS

APT.# | CITY

STATE/PROV. | ZIP/POSTAL CODE

EMAIL ☐ Please check this box if you would like to receive newsletters and promotional emails from Harlequin Enterprises ULC and its affiliates. You can unsubscribe anytime.

If offer card is missing write to: Harlequin Reader Service, P.O. Box 1341, Buffalo, NY 14240-8531 or visit www.ReaderService.com ▼

**BUSINESS REPLY MAIL**

FIRST-CLASS MAIL    PERMIT NO. 717    BUFFALO, NY

POSTAGE WILL BE PAID BY ADDRESSEE

**HARLEQUIN READER SERVICE**

PO BOX 1341

BUFFALO NY 14240-8571

NO POSTAGE
NECESSARY
IF MAILED
IN THE
UNITED STATES

He would give her everything they could have had then.

Because now triumph burned in his veins, and need burned in his gut, and he needed her. He needed her more than he needed to breathe.

He needed her more than he needed anything.

Like atonement.

Like redemption.

He took her hand and escorted her from the room.

When they were outside the palace, Eloise did something entirely unexpected. She threw her arms around his neck, and kissed him.

# CHAPTER EIGHT

ELOISE COULD NOT explain what was happening to her. She couldn't explain the feeling that was fizzing through her veins.

But she felt like she was ready to crawl out of her own skin. She felt like she was ready for something. For something big. For something changing. Altering.

She needed him. As she had felt when she was eighteen, but this time that burned brighter and hotter.

This time she burned brighter and hotter.

Incandescent.

Rage.

She was so angry. For the shame the King had made her feel all these years. For the way she had been written about. She had tried to push all that aside, to reconcile it. But it was wrong, and it had hurt. She had been called a whore countless times, wrapped in the language of smug men wielding pens and trying to sell clicks.

And she had never let herself be angry. She had tried to move on. She had tried to let it go, but here she was, back in the thick of everything, and she could not let it go. She did not feel placid and healed and normal. She did not feel like a lazy day gardening. She felt like a thwarted warrior who needed only a sword so that she could take it out and cut off the head of her accuser.

She was furious. And right then she did want revenge. Right now she wanted satisfaction for all the things that she had been through. For the life spent ignored, for the girl that she had been walking these palace halls, for the young woman she had become who had fallen in love with Vincenzo only to be cruelly rejected. Who had been paid off by the one person she'd cared about, and he hadn't believed in her any more than anyone else. Who'd had to forge a life by herself. Who had only ever been able to find contentment by herself, and never with another person. And certainly never in the arms of another person.

It was hell.

And she felt like she was burning.

She had tried. She had tried so hard to be… Above it. But right now she was in it. And she was being roasted in these flames, and she wanted to burn more. Burn brighter. Burn until it was not only anger. Burn until she was not just a victim. She wanted to burn it all away. All of it. And so, without thinking, she kissed him. And it was everything she had ever imagined. More than that kiss out on the dance floor, which had sparked something in her. More than touching his chest during their dance lesson this morning—had it really been this morning? She could hardly believe it. More than anything. Ever.

It was all him. It always had been. And maybe tonight was about reclaiming something. Reclaiming something for her own. Reclaiming a piece of her that had never experienced satisfaction.

Maybe that's what it was.

And so she kissed him. He put his hand on the back of her head and held her close. Angled his head so that he could take the kiss deeper. And when his tongue touched hers, it was gasoline to the lit match that was Eloise.

They were standing there in front of the palace, and it might as well be a burning building behind them. Ready to explode with the powder keg they had set off there. And still they were kissing. Absurdly, and perhaps appropriately.

"Let's go," he growled against her mouth.

He growled.

He did want her.

And everything else could wait. All of the complicated feelings she had about tonight, all of her concerns for the future. All of it could wait until tonight was over. Because tonight she felt beautiful, and it didn't feel like it had teeth. Didn't feel like the cost of her beauty was her dignity or her agency. Didn't feel like her beauty could only exist if it took the shape her mother tried to force her into.

She felt both in and out of control in the most glorious, delicious way. And she wanted to claim it. As she staked a claim on herself and on him. He had been a wound. An old wound that had lived deep inside her, not because she didn't understand that their age difference at the time had made it perfectly reasonable that he had rejected her. It was that she had felt like she had revealed a part of herself, for the first time, to another person, and she had been rejected. She had felt fragile all these years. And now she felt... Reborn. Like she was reclaiming something that had been twisted and perverted, taken from her.

Tonight she felt giddy with her excitement over him. With the hope of what it might mean.

No, not a future together. He had made it abundantly clear that was never going to happen for him. And as for her...

She could not tie herself to this family. To this place. This was the end of it. Her eyes filled with tears, because she did not want to think of that. So she leaned in and kissed him again, and she pushed all thoughts of the future away.

They got into the limo, and he pulled her onto his lap. She put her thighs on either side of his and kissed him, uncertain where her confidence came from. Where her reckless abandon had come from.

She rocked her hips against the hard ridge of his arousal and she ignited.

She was slick and hot and ready for him, and a childhood crush had not prepared her for the desire she would feel as a woman.

No. It had not. "We still have to get into my penthouse," he growled. "Or I would strip you naked now."

The dark promise sent a thrill through her entire body. She would not be opposed to that. Not really. They could have the driver go around the block and he could take her here, right in the back of the car. They wouldn't have to pause to think; they wouldn't have to pause for breath. They wouldn't have to pause for anything, and that was what she wanted. Because thought felt like the enemy right now. She didn't want thoughts. She wanted feelings. Nothing more than the deep, intense feelings that existed between them. The unending desire that he had built inside her. It felt magical. And few things in her life ever felt magical.

She nearly laughed.

Because she could remember when she had been a girl, and she had thought that moving to the palace meant she was a princess.

There was nothing half so terrible as a nightmare adjacent to a fantasy. She knew, because she had lived it. She had never been a princess. She had been a ghost.

A ghost in her own life. A ghost in the life of those around her, and she would not do it. Not now. Not anymore.

And so she rolled her hips forward and reached between them, undoing the button on his pants and undoing the zipper as well, reaching her hand inside and gripping the hot, hard evidence of his desire for her.

His breath hissed through his teeth, and she marveled her own boldness.

But she was not a girl. She might not have practical experience of men and sex, but she knew all about it. She had read plenty of books that described the act in glorious metaphor and had seen quite a few TV series that had presented it in less than metaphorical visuals.

She knew that it was all right for a woman to be bold. In fact, it was appreciated.

And she knew what to do to follow her own desire. That felt somehow miraculously like a gift. Like an inbuilt sort of magic she hadn't known was there.

His head fell back onto the seat, his breath hissing through his lips. And she pushed herself off his lap, down onto the floor of the limo. She looked up at him, at the strong, hard column of his arousal.

She leaned in, flicking her tongue over the head of him. And he reached back, grabbing her hair and guiding her movements as she took him deep between her lips, sliding her tongue over his hardened length.

She was lost in it. In the glory. In her power.

For here she was on her knees with the most vulnerable part of him in her mouth. And he was at her mercy.

It didn't matter that she was less experienced. It didn't matter that she was younger. Here, they were equals. Here, on her knees before the Prince, perhaps she was even the one in charge of things.

It was a heady discovery. A deep, intense experience that she hadn't known she had wanted. But hadn't she spent all of her life feeling helpless? Surrounded by people with more money, more power and more powers of manipulation than she would ever have.

She was in charge now. She was.

He growled, bucking his hips upward, the hard length of him touching the back of her throat, and she steeled herself against that surge of power. And found that she loved it. Because it spoke of his lack of control. Because it spoke of his need for her.

She continued to pleasure him like that, until the limo pulled up to the front of the building. He looked down at her, his black eyes glittering.

"Maybe you should tell him to go around the block," she said, sliding her tongue from his base to his tip.

The tension in his neck was evident, the tendons

there standing out, the tension in his jaw live with electricity.

"No," he said.

He righted his trousers, putting himself away and pulling her back up to the seat.

"We will finish this properly."

And she hated the underlying truth in those words, because what he was not saying was that they would finish it in a bed because tonight would be the only night they ever had.

Because this was their only moment.

It made her feel a sense of profound grief, and she couldn't understand it.

She didn't want to understand it.

He got out of the car, then reached in, taking her hand and drawing her out onto the street as though she had not just been tasting him intimately. They looked for all the world like a proper couple who had not been engaged in sex acts in the back of a car.

It gave her a secret, giddy thrill.

It made her feel like she never had before.

Because she had given herself that quiet life, had disappeared into her garden and her flowers.

Those flowers that were simply beautiful as they grew and didn't have to strive for it. Those flowers that were not victimized for their beauty.

She had done it because it was healing, but her version of healing had had a cost. It was far too quiet. At the end of all things, it felt too sedate.

At the end of everything, what she had done was sand all the hard edges off her life, but with that she had taken the excitement. The thrill.

In truth, she had never really had a thrill. In truth, all of her life had been decided by others. There had been pain, there had been grief and sadness and neglect. There had been danger.

But no one had ever thrown her a birthday party. She had been surrounded by evidence that the capacity for lavish celebrations existed, but none had ever been wasted on her.

Not a kind word had ever been thrown her way.

Living amongst all that wealth… And no one had ever distributed even the smallest bit to her. She was fed, and she was clothed.

But she did not have beautiful Christmas trees and Christmas presents.

Because she was not a princess. And she never had been.

And so for this night, to seize the thrill of it all… It seemed worth it. But she mourned already that it could not go on.

At least she had a quiet life to return to. A safe life.

At least she had that.

The elevator ride was a study in torture, and they stood with just a scant amount of space between their bodies. And she did her best to breathe. To breathe in and out and to stop her thoughts. Her body was rioting with desire. She could still taste him on her tongue, and she was slick between her thighs with the anticipation of what was to come.

The elevator doors opened, and he walked out ahead of her and extended his hand, as he had done out on the street, but this time they were not going out into public. This time he was beckoning her into his lair.

This time he was inviting her to a private night of sin, and she was going to accept. She reached out, and her fingertips brushed his. A shudder went down her spine. The desire that was growing inside her was almost pain.

He drew her out, his dark eyes never leaving hers. Her mouth went dry.

No, it wasn't almost pain. Now it was pain. A deep, aching emptiness, and the desire to be filled by him.

She wanted him. She might be a virgin, but she knew full well what was going to happen here, and that she would receive it with great relish. She wasn't concerned about the pain.

Pain was familiar to her. And pain passed. That was one thing she had learned. You could live through unimaginable emotional pain. Betrayal, fear. You just had to find a way to get through the moment. A bit of physical pain didn't concern her at all.

It was amazing, really. That she had no nerves. That she didn't feel a sense of worry over what she did not know. Because she was with Vincenzo. And everything would be fine. That knowledge echoed deep within her soul, and she could not have explained it to anyone, let alone herself.

But it was Vincenzo.

The man she had fallen in love with when she was a teenager. The man she had never forgotten.

The man she had always wanted. This… This was inevitable in a way that she could never explain.

It felt right.

Sad in a way, but in a way that she was determined not to think about. Because this was their night.

The culmination of all that she had felt for him from the time she was a girl.

Vincenzo.

And then he swept her into his arms, and he kissed her, with a deep, unyielding need that stoked a fire down in her belly and made her feel like she was the flame itself.

She stood back away from him; she needed to do this. She reached around behind herself and grabbed the zipper tab on the revealing dress that she had worn all evening and unzipped it. Let it fall down to her waist, let it reveal her bare breasts. She needed to do this. To choose to reveal her body to him.

To stand proud in it.

Because it was the evidence of the shape that her life had taken. Of the things that she loved. Of the fact that she enjoyed baking bread and eating it too.

That she liked cakes, and always had. That she also worked outside in the sun, and had freckles on her arms and shoulders from being out in it. That her nails were short because you could not garden with long fingernails, at least not nicely and easily.

This was the Eloise that she had chosen to be. And now she was choosing to give herself to him.

She pushed the dress down over her hips, leaving herself standing there in only her glorious, gold shoes and a pair of gold panties. She knew, because she had looked at herself in the mirror, that they made a slight dent in her hips, and she had known a moment of insecurity about that. Because it revealed her body was not perfectly taut or toned.

But then she looked at his face and saw the hunger there. She did not feel regretful about anything. About herself.

She took a step toward him, and she saw a muscle in his jaw jump.

"You are beautiful," he rasped, the words scraping over his throat.

Her cheeks heated.

"I'm glad you think so."

"I would never say that your body is made for sex. Not when it clearly accomplishes so many other wonderful things. But I do believe that sex…with me… may be one of its highest purposes."

She should not appreciate that. But she did.

She stopped, and she put her hand on his chest.

"Only if you concede that your body was definitely made for sex. And most especially with me." His lips curved into a smile, and it made her stomach dip. Because how often did this man smile? So rarely. If ever.

She began to undo the buttons on his shirt, slowly, and there was an increased thrill to seeing his chest when she was the one uncovering it. It had been glorious when he had come in shirtless, and she had danced with him only this morning, but this...

This was unmistakably sexual. An unmistakable expression of their need for one another. She moved her hands over the hard planes of his chest, his stomach, then slid them back up to his shoulders, pushing his shirt and jacket down onto the floor.

He was glorious. Just standing there in a low-slung pair of black pants, all his hard-cut muscles on display.

He was physical perfection. In the classic sense. A man who seemed carved from rock rather than flesh, and yet he was hot to the touch, and she could not deny that he was every inch a man. He made her mouth water.

And she had thought that she wanted to lick him. So now she would.

She leaned in, kissing his chest, then pressing the flat of her tongue there, drawing it over his nipple and up his neck, before biting the edge of his jaw.

And he moved, grabbing hold of her, taking her

wrists and pinning them behind her back, down at the base of her spine.

"Little minx."

"Maybe."

She didn't feel like herself. Or rather, she did. She felt like herself unfettered, even as he held her there captive.

She had wondered what it might be like to live in a moment where she didn't carry pain or baggage from the past. Where she didn't carry inhibition, and she seemed to be living in that fantasy.

For everything just felt right. Everything felt free. And so did she.

He kissed her, holding her captive as he did so. And then he lifted her up off the ground and carried her back to his bedroom.

He deposited her at the center of the bed and reached out, hooking his finger through the waistband of her panties and dragging them down her legs. Then he took hold of her ankles, undid the delicate buckles on her shoes, one by one, slid them off and discarded them on the floor.

"Sit back against the pillows," he commanded. "And spread your legs."

For a moment, she knew embarrassment, because it was a frank command. And she did not know that she could withstand it.

"Spread them," he repeated, and so she found herself obeying, sliding back and leaning against the pillows on the headboard, parting her thighs, even though she felt as if there was a magnet between them trying to get her to put them back shut. To conceal herself.

It was one thing to stand before him bare, and imagine herself a classical painting, but quite another to do something so openly sexual.

This was not the kind of thing you could walk into a museum and see.

This was something else altogether.

But she did it. And when she saw the effect that it had on him, when she could see the outline of his arousal through the fabric of his pants, her embarrassment faded away. And she found herself unconsciously moving her hand toward the heart of herself, drawing her finger slowly through her own slick folds.

"Dammit, Eloise," he ground out. "This is not going to last as long as I wanted it to."

"But we have all night," she said, her breath coming in short bursts as her arousal began to reach a fever pitch.

The need for him combined with the teasing touch of her own fingers.

And the view of his desire for her.

"Yes," he agreed.

He kicked his shoes and socks off, and then moved his hands to his belt buckle, undoing it slowly before pushing his pants down his lean hips and revealing his flesh to her.

She arched her hips up off the bed, beseeching.

Because she was so hungry for him.

His lips curved slightly.

He wrapped his masculine hand around his own desire, squeezing himself, and then he made his way to the bed, still holding his arousal in hand. He slid his hand around the back of her head and forced her head upward, kissing her. Then he moved between her thighs and replaced the touch of her hand with the head of him. He slid it back and forth through her slick folds, and she shuddered, that hollow sensation there growing more pronounced. Growing wider.

"Please," she whispered.

"Not yet," he growled. He moved down her body, kissing her breasts, sucking one nipple into his mouth before turning his attention to the other one. Then he kissed his way down her stomach, until his face was scant inches from the most intimate part of her, his hands on her hips. Then he started to lick her. He was not delicate in the strokes he made against her body. He was decisive. Firm. The flat of his tongue moving over the most sensitized part of her. And then he moved his lips to that centralized bundle of nerves and sucked it in deep.

She screamed. Her climax broke over her in a wave, pounding against her, never-ending.

And when he came back to her, kissed her, let her taste her own desire, there was no fear in her.

Only need.

The need for him that she'd had for so many years.

This man who had felt like the other half of her soul at one time.

Leaving him had felt like losing herself.

But he was here now.

And he was there, between her thighs again, the blunt head of him now probing the entrance to her body. And she could feel herself stretching, could feel a slight bit of pain.

Then he growled and thrust into her in one smooth stroke, pain and pleasure bursting behind her eyes, for this was what she had wanted. More than anything. This was the answer to the need in her, and while there was pain there, it was offset by the deep sense of satisfaction that she felt. And she understood it. She understood why women did this even though it hurt.

Because it hurt not to. Because it was the only way to find true satisfaction.

Because there was no other answer.

He looked at her, his expression strange, but it faded. And then he began to move. Building the desire in her stroke by glorious stroke.

Impossibly, she felt need begin to build inside of her again. And when it broke over her, he went right along with her, growling out his pleasure as he found his own release. As he spilled himself inside of her.

And when it was over, he lay beside her, stroking her face.

"You should've told me," he said.

"I should've told you what?"

"You either have not been with a man for a very long time, or you have never been with a man at all."

She closed her eyes. She could lie. She could lie to protect herself. But why? This was tonight.

And they got to have tonight. And why should there be any lies between them?

"I have not been with a man," she said. "Not with anyone."

"No, Eloise," he said. "I was appalling to you."

"Yes," she said. "You were. But I'm used to that."

"I hate that even more. That it did not affect you because I'm just one of the many people who have treated you cruelly."

"The world is cruel, Vincenzo. And we either hide from it as I have done, or we learn to become cruel in it, as you have done. At least you fight for the right things. You try. You have honor."

And she realized as she said the words, just how true they were. That this was why it could only be one night. For Vincenzo had chosen his path, and she had chosen hers. And tonight they were able to meet in this bright place of glory. Tonight, they were able to meet at this place of pleasure. Where neither the world nor either of them needed to be cruel.

But she would have to go back. Because she had chosen her way, and he had chosen his.

And she had to admit to herself that his way... It was hard and sharp. Like living in a battlefield, but it at least helped people. What did her method do? It did nothing. It did not protect anyone else.

It made her feel ashamed.

But they had tonight. And she would not let anything else matter.

"Why have you not been with another man?"

"You know why not," she said. "You know why."

"My father."

"It's part of it. But I never felt like my body was right. And I never felt like it was mine. And I was afraid... I was afraid of becoming my mother. She has made terrible choices in the pursuit of men. In the pursuit of her desire for them. Or for what they can give her, and I never wanted that. You must understand, what happened between the two of us made me question myself in a very deep way. And I did not wish to question that. I did not wish to find myself lacking in that way."

"The very fact that you have a concern about that proves that you are not your mother."

"Perhaps."

"It doesn't matter. Tonight you are mine."

She smiled. "Yes. Tonight I'm yours.

They made love all night and slept in between. At one point he got up and made them a platter of fruit, cheese and honey. All the things that he already knew that she loved, and it made her ache. Because this could not last. Because she could not stay with him. With her Vincenzo. She had to get away from here. She had to go back to the safe space that she had created for herself. But they had tonight. And it had been glorious. That would be enough.

It would have to be.

When the sun rose up over the mountains, she dressed in the clothing that was hers and sneaked out of the penthouse. It did not take long for her to find a flight that would take her back to Virginia by way of England.

She turned her phone off so that when Vincenzo discovered that she was gone he would not be able to contact her. Because if he did… She would not be able to be strong.

# CHAPTER NINE

WHEN HE HAD awakened to find that Eloise was gone, it had come as a shock to him. A shock that had faded with the passage of these many months, especially as the media storm that he had brought down upon his father, and on Arista, had had some unexpected results.

His father had abdicated. And fled before legal proceedings could be taken up against him. Whether or not he had taken Cressida St George along with him was a mystery, but she had vanished as well.

Leaving Vincenzo on the cusp of being crowned King. His coronation would coincide with the new year. Though it was merely a formality, as he was even now acting the part of ruler.

It gave him little time to ponder Eloise. But he did. In those quiet moments when there was nothing but the breeze and he thought of roses.

It was an impossibility, anyway. The two of them. An impossibility that they should ever have anything more than that single night.

It was perfect, poetic in many ways. As if they had somehow consummated the vengeance itself.

And yet he dreamed of her.

And he wanted no other woman. Though he told himself there was no time for women anyway.

He was rearranging a country.

He was not going to plunge them straight into democracy, but rather he was establishing oversight. Parliament. He would not abolish the monarchy overnight, for there was no practicality there.

The people were used to being ruled with an iron fist, and when it came to restrictions, Vincenzo was opening the floodgates.

There were many older citizens, however, who wondered at the security if they did not have a king.

And Vincenzo was happy to see that everything ran the way that he thought it should, and that everyone felt secure.

He was thankful, also, for his friends from Oxford, who had been his lifeline through all of this.

Rafael, bastard though he was, in every sense of the word, had been the acting Regent of his nation for years, waiting for his younger brother, the true heir, to come into majority.

Jag was well established in his own country, and Zeus was god of all he surveyed. Though he was not the ruler of his country as yet, he certainly behaved as though he ran the world.

It was not unusual for them to clear their schedules and fly to the nearest major city to meet up for a drink or two. Even less unusual for them to make video calls to one another. He felt privileged to be surrounded by them as advisors. Though he often thought it funny, given the hell they had raised in their youths. Age, he thought, came for everyone.

So it was not entirely unexpected when his computer chimed, and he answered, that the first face that popped up was Rafael. Followed by Zeus and then Jag.

"It's late here," Jag said.

"Apologies," Rafael said, but he did not sound at all sorry.

He could see that Rafael was in his study, a fire roaring behind him. It was cold in his mountainous country near Spain, as it was in Arista.

"You've never been apologetic a day in your life," Zeus said. "It's one of the things I like about you."

Rafael waved a hand, dismissing them. Then his black eyes met Vincenzo's through the screen. "You have not seen," he said.

"Seen what?"

"I knew it. For if you had seen it, you would've phoned us. Or, at least would've looked like thunder when you answered."

"I always look like thunder. The cost of figuring out how to repair a country so badly managed."

"No," Rafael said. "This is worse than the state of your country."

"What?"

Rafael picked up a newspaper and held it up. It took a moment for it to come into focus on the screen, but when it did…

"What is the meaning of this?"

"Why, it looks as though your lover is round with child," Zeus said, looking darkly amused. "So much for all of your proclamations regarding the ending of your line. It seems that your seed is prodigious."

"I will thank you to not speak of my seed," Vincenzo said, continuing to stare at the image before him.

For it was indeed Eloise. At a grocery store, with a very clear and obvious baby bump beneath her sweater.

"Why is this…"

But the headline made it all clear. The former lover of King Vincenzo, who had disappeared seven months prior without a word after dropping bombshells regarding the previous King of Arista, was now looking about as pregnant as one might be had they conceived during that time. So of course the speculation was that she carried the heir to the throne of Arista.

*She carried the heir to the throne of Arista.*

The truth of it hit him hard.

He had failed.

He had made one vow. He had said that he would not carry on his father's line, and that bastard yet lived, and he was likely bringing a child into the world. It filled him with rage.

"No," he said. "This must be... It must be doctored."

"You did not sleep with the delectable woman that you brought to help destroy your father?" Jag asked.

"That is beside the matter. I have slept with many women, and none of them have ended up carrying my child."

"Yes, but did you use a condom?" Rafael asked.

"Excuse me?"

"A condom," Zeus said. "They've been around for quite some time. Known by many names. French letters. Surely even in your little backward country you are familiar with the concept of keeping it under wraps."

"I..."

He had not used a condom. And he was only just realizing this. He had been... It had been an intense night. Filled with the revelations of the day and the rather unpleasant business of the ball. And he had been swept away. Just as she had been. But she was a virgin. He should've...

"Yeah," Zeus said. "No condom. Excellent."

"You must marry her," Rafael said.

"I'm sorry, am I taking orders from you now?"

"No," Rafael said. "But as the bastard in this group of legitimized men, I feel I must speak to my own experience. The Crown was denied to me. Because my father would not marry my mother. And here I am, doing all the work, planning my brother's wedding, in fact, so that he might take the throne. Managing all the things that come with it, as if I am a glorified nanny, all for want of legal documentation between my parents. I could've been king. Instead of a nanny."

"It is my will that none should be king," Vincenzo said.

"So abolish the monarchy. Carry on as you intended," Jag said. "There is no reason for you to change your plans. But Rafael is right. A real man does not impregnate a woman and allow her to go unwed."

"We do not all live in the Dark Ages," Zeus said. "I don't know. You could set her up in a very nice home. Adjacent to yours, if you ever plan on visiting the child. Though, children are quite boring."

"Thank you," Vincenzo said. "For your concerns regarding the entertainment factor of the child that I may have created. However, whether or not I find it amusing to become a father is irrelevant. If I am to become one… Then I will do as I must."

"You will marry her," Rafael said.

"Not because you told me to," Vincenzo said.

"Petulant," Zeus said.

"Hardly. As if you would obey the dictates of that asshole."

"Absolutely not," Zeus said. "I cannot be tamed. By anyone. But, I use condoms. So."

"God help you when you meet a vixen who matches the appeal of Eloise St. George."

It was foolish to even attempt to defend himself, and yet he did.

"I have met any number of vixens," Zeus said. "Minxes, scarlet women and temptresses. And still. No bastards."

"Marry her quickly," Rafael said. "We will all be at your wedding."

"We'd better be *in* the wedding," Zeus said.

"I should think so," Jag said. "It is the only wedding we are likely to take part in."

And all Vincenzo could think was that he would be incredibly, darkly amused if any one of them ended up in the position where they were forced to marry. "Just don't make it around the new year," Rafael said. "It is my brother's wedding."

"Yes," Zeus said. "He is marrying that fresh-faced little princess from Santa Castelia. She is quite delectable."

Rafael's face turned to stone. "She is barely twenty-two years of age. I would prefer you keep your opinions on my future sister-in-law and her beauty to yourself."

There was a thread of steel in his voice that was always present, but it was much more intense than usual.

He had not given full credit to the rather unfair nature of the situation Rafael found himself in.

Because of course, he was a placeholder. For his younger brother, who he must herd through life as if he was his son.

All after their father gave no thought at all to Rafael himself.

But Rafael's problems were of no real concern to him right now. The biggest issue was the fact that he was going to be a father.

*He was going to be a father.*

He had never wanted this. He had sworn that he would not…

He was here in Arista, on the cusp of keeping his promise to his father. Working to dismantle everything.

But Eloise was carrying his baby. And that changed everything. Eloise, who he had not been able to stop thinking of since their time together. Eloise.

"I must charter a private jet to Virginia."

"When?" Zeus asked.

"Tonight."

Eloise was sitting at the kitchen table, solemnly looking around at all her decorations. She had imagined that when she was an adult she might have a different sort of holiday season. That she would decorate festively and cheerfully and capture the magic of Christmas that she had always missed as a girl.

She had always done her house up beautifully, and yet it still never felt… Magic. But even now, nursing a broken heart, she felt a tingling of magic. Because by next Christmas she would have a child to share the holiday with.

The thought made her heart nearly overflow.

She had been terrified, ever since she had taken that pregnancy test and it had come back positive. But she had known... She had known that she wanted the child. She had also known with perfect clarity that Vincenzo did not. He had vowed never to have an heir. It meant something to him. That promise.

Vincenzo was on a path. And nothing would change his mind about that path. Nothing. She didn't want their child to be a source of contention. She had returned to her quiet life, and that was a gift. She had her cottage; it was paid for. And she wanted the baby. She wanted to be a mother. And she had not fully realized what that would mean until this moment. Sitting there in her house surrounded by the Christmas decorations that had never really created the feeling in her that she wanted to have.

Holidays in the palace had been—as had everything—for the enjoyment of the adults. There had been parties she was not allowed to attend and gifts that had not been for her.

She had never had anyone to share it with.

She had never had family to sit by the Christmas tree with. And now she would. And her child... She would throw them birthday parties and Christmas celebrations. She would delight in their achievements and comfort them when they failed. She would do for her child what no one had ever done for her.

And there was something hopeful in that. In knowing that she could change something about the world. And knowing that she could take a little piece of the hurt inside of herself and transform it into something different. Into something new.

No, she could never have the relationship with her mother that she might have wished for as a child, but she could be the kind of mother that she had wished for. She would have another person in her life that she could love and...

Well, very much of her had wished that she could love Vincenzo but... This was better. It was.

She would raise the child far away from Arista. Far away from the palace, and all that pain. It would be better. She would be better.

No. She couldn't have Vincenzo.

But that was all right.

She had accepted that. Before she had gotten into his bed. She wished, just slightly, that she might have thought a little more clearly about the consequences of their joining. But...

Now? Now she felt happy. Even now, sitting there by herself with the snow falling outside the window...

There was a knock at the door. Skerret leaped onto the table and knocked her ball of yarn off onto the floor.

"Skerret," she scolded.

The cat jumped down, startling again when there was another knock on the door.

She got up, and she walked over to the door, looking out the side window. Her heart fell down to her feet.

Because standing there on the doorstep, snowflakes collecting on the shoulder of his dark wool coat, was Vincenzo.

Oh, she didn't know what to do. She hadn't wanted him to know about this… She glanced down at her rounded stomach. But she couldn't avoid him. He was here.

It didn't matter. She would simply face it. It was her decision after all. She was pregnant, and she wanted the baby.

She took a deep breath and opened the door. But what she was about to say died on her lips. Because she had forgotten how beautiful he was. Or maybe it was simply that a mere memory could not hold within it the intensity and brilliance that was Vincenzo Moretti.

"Hi," she said.

Well, that was just perfect. That was not at all what she had meant to say.

He looked down at her stomach, then back up at her. "It is true," he said.

"What's true?"

From the interior pocket of his jacket he took a folded-up newspaper and held it out toward her.

And then she recognized herself. Standing in front of a rack of candy bars, with her baby bump clear and visible. And the headline read: King's Lover Pregnant with Heir?

"Oh, no," she said. "I don't... Vincenzo, I don't know how they got this..."

"Do not tell me the baby is not mine, *cara mia*. For we both know that it is. You were a virgin when you came to my bed, and I hardly think that you leaped straight from my bed into a different one."

"How do you know?" She scowled, indignant at his assumption. "For all you know, I decided sex is actually quite fun and I should like to have more of it. Maybe I went straight from your bed to someone else's. I did leave very quickly." She was practically breathing fire. He'd thought all of this about her easily before, why not now?

Standing there in a rage as if she'd betrayed him, when she knew damned well, as did he, that he'd emphatically stated he did not want a child. As if she'd taken something from him when he had said from the beginning he wanted nothing to do with it.

"Do not play games, Eloise," he said. "I'm not amenable to them."

"Well, what you are or aren't amenable to is my highest concern, Vincenzo."

"Come with me."

She should have known that if he found out he would be inflexible, obnoxious and demanding. On account of the fact he was inflexible, obnoxious and demanding.

"I cannot come with you," she said. "I have a Christmas tree. And a cat."

"Is the cat not outdoors?"

"No. When it began to snow I brought Skerret in."

His lips flattened into a stark line. "That is a ridiculous name for a cat."

"Well, it just kind of... It fits her. Because she gets scared very easily. And also she is sort of slinky like a ferret. And so she's a Skerret."

"It is still ridiculous."

She was pregnant, he had come to take her away and they were debating the merits of her cat's name. "I can't go with you," she said forcefully.

"You can't or you won't?"

"It amounts to the same thing. And anyway, you said you didn't want a child. You in fact vowed never to have one."

"I did. But you are having one. So... It does not matter what I said."

"Yes, it does," she said. "Vincenzo, you can pretend it doesn't matter but it does. Look, you don't have to do anything with this child. I am prepared to care for him or her myself."

"You don't know what you're having?"

"No. I declined to find out. I wanted to be surprised. I know it sounds strange, but I'm very happy. The idea of being a mother... I didn't know that I wanted it. I had told myself that I would be better off living a quiet life by myself. But now... I quite like the idea of sharing it with someone. It pleases me. I'm very... I'm very content with the way things are turning out. You have to trust me. I... I'm not unhappy."

"You mistake me," he said, stepping into the cottage and filling the space. She had forgotten, too, how commanding his presence was. "I did not come here to see to your well-being, Eloise. I came here to claim my child. This is not a welfare check. This is a proposal. Or kidnap, if need be."

"A *proposal*?"

"You will marry me."

"That is a demand, not a proposal. And I will not," she said.

"You will," he said. "I am about to be King, and we must marry before my coronation or the child will be a bastard. Do you understand the implications of that?"

"I... I guess I don't. I... This isn't the Dark Ages. Surely that doesn't mean a thing."

"It does. It means he or she will not be able to inherit the throne."

"You did not want the throne to carry on," she said.

"I don't know what I want now," he said, shaking his head. "There was a way of things. That I had planned, and none of this fits into it. None of this is what I wanted. None of it is right. And yet it is what is. So I must adjust my plans accordingly, must I not?"

"I'm set to have Christmas here."

"It does not matter. You will come with me."

"Don't you want to know why I left?"

He looked as if she had slapped him.

"Why you left?"

"Yes. The morning after we… After we were together. Don't you want to know why I left?"

"Why then? As you are surely intent on telling me."

"I left because I could not stand the idea of…being in Arista any longer. I do not want to be in the palace. All of it, the royal protocol, the location, the walls themselves are nothing more than a terrible memory for me. And it is not something that I can…fathom living with for the rest of my life. Vincenzo, this is my home. And in it I made a place for myself, and I do not wish to go back to being that sad girl lost in a royal life that she was never meant to live."

"I am not my father," he whispered.

"I didn't say that you were. But that does not change the fact that I do not feel at home there. Nor do I want to."

She had just been sitting there, feeling excited about her future. About what she might have with her child. She had been imagining the simple, quiet life where they did not have to consider anyone. Where they did not have to conform, or hide in the shadows.

The very idea of returning and marrying Vincenzo… And he was to be King! It was everything she didn't want. It was so many connections, so much responsibility. It was a nightmare.

"No. I cannot."

"Come back with me," he said.

"No, Vincenzo."

"You must come back with me," he said. "Or I will have no choice but to take the child."

"You wouldn't." She searched his face, tried to put aside her own fear, her own anger and see what on earth he was thinking. Feeling. He'd said he didn't want this, and yet here he was. One thing she knew was Vincenzo was a man driven by his own code of honor, consumed by it, and it didn't matter if she could make sense of it or not. When he decided something, it was the way of things. "You don't want the child," she reminded him. "You said as much yourself."

"I said I didn't want a child. Now there will be one. And that is simply the way of it. I am not turning away from my responsibility. I will not do it. I am a man who knows what is right. And I will do it. I will do my duty. In this as in all things." His voice sounded shattered, and it was the only thing on earth keeping her from lashing out at him entirely.

The only thing that was pressing her to go with him.

"So you really will blackmail me, then?"

"If I have to. I was always willing to, Eloise. That must've been clear."

"I'm bringing my cat," she said.

He looked down at the small creature, the disdain he felt for the little scrappy tabby apparent. "It shall not be loose on the plane."

"Of course not," she said. "What a silly suggestion. She cannot be loose on the plane. It would terrify her. She will be in a crate."

"And what else?"

"What do you care what else I want? It does not matter to you."

"It may shock you, Eloise, but your misery is not actually my goal. What I want is my child."

"Why?"

"Is it not the most natural thing in the world to want your child?"

She stared at him. "You and I both know that it is not. You cannot simply expect that someone will. Did my mother really want me?"

"Eloise…"

She shook her head. "You might be able to take the baby from me, but you cannot force me to marry you. And then the child will not be legitimate."

"Eloise…"

"No. I know that I don't have a lot of power here, but I have had so little choice in my life, Vincenzo. Surely you must want to do better for me than my own mother did. Surely you must want more than to hide me away in this place. Surely I deserve more than that."

"What is it you want?" he said.

It came to her in a moment, because the truth was, it would be... A wonderful thing for her child to know its father.

It was only her fears of that palace, of that life, that truly held her back.

"Make me a beautiful Christmas there at the palace. Show me that there's something there other than what I remember. Other than that dreadful... awful empty feeling that I always get in the palace. You show me. Show me that there is something else. Show me that there can be more. That there can be happiness."

"As you wish," he said. But he looked angry. And he did not look happy at all.

"Gather your cat," he said.

"And my Christmas tree," she said. Because on this she would not budge. And maybe she was just throwing out a ridiculous thing she did not think that Vincenzo could or would accomplish. But if she was going to subject herself to being married to him, if she was going to go back there, she needed him to try. But as she packed her things to go, her heart nearly cracked with an unimaginable grief at the thought of leaving this place.

This safety.

And then Vincenzo went into her living room,

picked the tree up and put it over his shoulder. Three ornaments dropped on the floor. "Be careful with that," she said.

"You told me you wanted to bring your tree. I cannot guarantee the manner in which it will arrive."

"I don't…"

"The plane is waiting. I will drive us there. And I will strap your tree to the roof."

"You really will?"

"Yes. Make your commands of me, and I will show you that I am equal to whatever task you assign. You asked me once if I wanted a quiet life. The truth of the matter is, I do not get to choose that. Because of my birth. Because of who my father is.

"The same is true for our child. And I do not want to limit their choices. And you…"

She nodded slowly. Because she knew. She knew she had a responsibility to her child. To their child. To doing what was best for them. No matter what. It was the one thing that his father and her mother had not been able to do. They had not been able to think of anyone else. They had thought only of themselves. And she could cling to her quiet life, her desire to stay away from Arista, but if she denied her child that which they were due by rights, if she denied her child the chance to know their father, when Vincenzo clearly wanted them? Then she would not be any better than her own mother. She simply could not do it. "Let's go."

And she knew she had no choice, not because he would pick her up like the tree and carry her out if she refused, but because there simply wasn't another choice. There simply wasn't.

## CHAPTER TEN

"You've done what?"

"I brought her back to the palace," he growled at his computer screen, and more specifically at Rafael.

"Did you kidnap her?" Zeus asked.

He shrugged. "Borderline."

"No one likes an indecisive kidnapping, Vincenzo," Zeus said.

"It was decisive enough. She is here, is she not?"

"Is she *marrying* you?" Rafael asked.

"Most likely."

"Most likely," Jag said. "That is…"

"Weak," Zeus said.

"Mmm," Rafael agreed.

"I cannot force her to marry me."

"Untrue," Jag said. "You can absolutely force her to marry you."

"Perhaps I do not *wish* to force her to marry me," he said.

"And why not?" Rafael said.

In truth, Vincenzo did quite want to force her to

marry him. When he had opened the door and seen her standing there, round and pregnant with his child he had… Well, he had picked up her Christmas tree, tossed it over his shoulder and brought it back with them to Arista! That was how strange and primal the response had been to seeing her like that. All he had known was that he would do anything to have her.

And yes, he actually would force her to marry him. If he had to.

"I am hoping to make her think it was her idea," he said.

"Oh," Zeus said. "That is smart."

"All she has asked is that I give her a Merry Christmas. She said if I can make her forget how difficult life was here at the palace when she was a child then she might be more… Amenable to staying with me."

"Buy her a pony, then," Zeus said.

"She did not ask for a pony."

Zeus looked at him as if he were insane. "All women want a pony."

"Then I will buy one. I will fill a stable with them for her. I will do it now."

"No one likes a reluctant gift giver," Zeus said.

"I do not care about any of this. Not ponies or Christmas."

His words landed in this group of men, for none of them had ever experienced the kind of happiness many associated with the holidays. They had never spoken of it, he simply knew.

Because they had never spoken of it.

That silence spoke volumes, like many other silences they had shared over the years.

"Let us send gifts," Rafael said. "To welcome her. Your new Queen."

He narrowed his gaze. "You don't need to do that."

"Yes, we do," Jag said. "I will have…" He snapped his fingers. "Yes. I have an idea. All will be sent tomorrow."

"I…"

"It is settled," Rafael said.

"Settled," Jag confirmed.

And then they vanished from the screen, and Vincenzo had a feeling he would not enjoy what came next.

He pushed the button on his desk and summoned the house manager. Who came quickly. "I wish to decorate the palace for Christmas. Every single room. From floor to ceiling. No expenses to be spared. The money is to be taken from my personal account. None of the money shall come from Arista."

"Your Majesty…"

"It is for Eloise. We must make this place beautiful for her. For she is to be my Queen," he said.

The manager looked delighted at that. "Your mother would be very pleased," the woman said.

"Perhaps," he said. "Perhaps not." He could not

imagine his mother being happy with him taking
Eloise as his bride. Considering the history of it all.

"Well I am pleased," the house manager said. "She
was always a nice girl. Very quiet. She never got the
childhood she deserved."

A strange pang of regret echoed in Vincenzo's
chest. "No," he said. "She didn't."

One thing he was utterly determined in—he had
been given a challenge to woo his princess in a specific way, and he would do it. He might not understand finer feelings. Might not be a man who knew
much about emotion. But he had a capable staff more
than able to ensure that any decorating needs might
be met.

And when it came to him personally… Well. He
knew about seduction. And that, he was confident,
would do the real work.

One thing he was certain of. Eloise would not be
able to resist him.

Let his friends send gifts. He would take a different approach.

Eloise didn't emerge from her room until late. She
was jet-lagged and had a terrible time sleeping the
previous night. She felt out of sorts and unhappy to
be back at the palace. Except… It was not that simple. It was not so simple as unhappy. Because in spite
of herself that was something that she wanted—to
be close to Vincenzo.

And she couldn't even be angry about the fact that he wanted their child.

No. What frightened her was the warmth that filled her at the thought. What frightened her was how much she wanted him to want their child.

When she emerged, she was met with a sight she had not expected.

It was magic. There were twinkling icicles hanging from the ceiling. Glittering rich green and red garlands swirled around every column, every balustrade. Every bannister. Wreaths were hung on every wall. There were gold candelabras with lit white taper candles casting a glow over the room.

The white palace was bedazzled. And trees. There were trees in every room. When she went into the dining room, there were four trees. One that stretched all the way to the ceiling, impossibly tall, two beside it a bit shorter. And in the center, her humble little tree that had come all the way from Virginia. She could not believe it. She simply couldn't believe it.

"I…"

"Good morning."

Elizabeth, the housekeeper, came into the room. She had always liked Elizabeth. There was a distance between them that had been ordered by the King, but she had never felt any chill coming from the other woman. And now, with the King gone, there was no reservation at all.

"Breakfast is set to be brought out upon your arrival. If you are ready?"

"Oh," she said. "Yes, I am."

"Coffee?"

"Herbal tea. Thank you." She had been quite happy that coffee didn't sound appealing, since strictly speaking you needed to limit it with pregnancy. She had thought it sounded unimaginable, but then she had attempted to drink the permitted one cup, and her stomach had turned.

All for the best.

"Right away."

She was only left alone for a moment when the double doors swung open, and one of the other members of staff, Pietro, came in and bowed with a flourish. "Ms. Eloise," he said. "Some gifts have been sent for you."

"Gifts?"

But she did not have to wait to see what that meant. For in through the doors came a veritable procession of staff. The first wave of them carrying bowls made of precious metals. Inside of them was dried fruit that sparkled like jewels. There were flowers, crystal bottles of perfume and woven rugs.

"From Sheikh Jahangir Hassan Umar Al Hayat," one of the men said, placing all of the bounty on the table in front of her. She sat down, overwhelmed. "Sent upon a hand-carved troika, for the lady to keep as her own."

"I... That's incredible."

"There is more."

Following that came another wave of staff, carrying baskets filled with olives, platters of cured meat, fruits and nuts.

"From Regent Rafael Navarro. The finest goods from his country." He handed her a stack of papers. "Also stocks," he said, "in the Regent's personal company. Should you need to make a bid for your freedom."

Eloise blinked. "Oh, well, that is very nice of him."

And then, at the very end, came a young woman, with a very small horse on a lead.

A horse.

"This is from Prince Zeus. With the message that, if at all possible. women should be given the world. But failing that, they ought to have a pony."

And she couldn't help it. It was ridiculous. She laughed. "How wonderful."

She looked up then and saw Vincenzo standing in the doorway looking like a thunderstorm.

"That bastard did not send a horse into my palace."

"Who?"

"Zeus," he said curling his lip. "I should've known he would do it."

"Who are these men who sent these gifts?"

"They are my..." He looked like the word he was about to say was causing him pain. "My friends."

Her eyes widened. "You have *friends*, Vincenzo?"

He arched a dark brow. "Endeavor to not sound so surprised about it, Eloise."

"Well, I am."

"They did not decorate the palace," he said. "I did. Well, I had it done."

"It's glorious," she beamed.

Her breakfast came out, which took the form of baskets full of pastries, butter, jam. It was all a bit much.

"I don't think I will be able to eat all of this," she said, considering the fruit baskets as well.

"I will help."

He sat down next to her. Next to her. This man who was King. It was such a small gesture, and yet it felt…

*Don't go romanticizing things like this.*

He wanted something from her, and he was willing to do anything to get it.

Yes. And she had wanted him to. So was it so bad that he was acting consistently in that manner? She swallowed. This was all she had wanted. All those years ago.

Well, she had wanted to kiss him. But there was something to this simple connection, here in the palace that… It felt intimate in a way. It felt right.

And no, it wasn't simple. It was complicated. All of this was complicated. There was a horse in the dining room for crying out loud.

"The horse should probably be taken outside," she said.

He nodded. "Have the pony taken to the stables," he ordered.

"I will go see her," she said. "After I'm finished."

"I do not think you have hurt the pony's feelings."

"I shouldn't like to hurt the pony's feelings."

"And how is... Skerret finding his new residence?"

"I believe he quite likes the back right side of my bed. Beneath it. He has not come out. But he has eaten. And has used his box."

"Good to know," he said.

"It will take some time to adjust. The palace is very large."

She didn't just mean the cat.

She stared at him, and she knew that he didn't really care how her cat was finding the adjustment. He was trying. She just wished she could understand more deeply why. Because he had said so firmly that he didn't want a child. And she could understand him making gestures toward it now out of a sense of duty, but the degree to which he seemed to be taking up the cause was... That was what she could not understand.

"Why do you want this child?"

"Because it is the right thing to do."

"Is it only important to do the right thing? In this way?"

"My father never did. Not on behalf of anyone

but himself. All I know is, in this life, I will make the decision to do what I know to be right. Whether I understand it, whether I want to… It is the path I have chosen."

"Right. That path of revenge."

"I removed my father from the throne, essentially. And now here I am, striving to set the nation on a better path, but grappling with the reality that the people are not completely happy with the idea of losing the monarchy. Even though they had no real love for my father. They like a symbol. And I am trying to affect change…"

"But it isn't as easy as coming in and ordering things to be done your way?"

"Do not sound so pleased about that, Eloise."

"I'm not. Actually… Vincenzo, you must know one wonderful thing about going off and having my simple life is that I have not been responsible for anyone else. Skerret. She is the only thing I've been responsible for all this time, other than my own happiness. And that is very easy. It is very easy. What you must do… It isn't. You are beholden to an entire nation, and I do not envy you that position. I never have. I was so happy to leave Arista. So happy to escape all of this. But you are right. There are other things to consider. I cannot face the idea of our child growing up in this palace as it was for us."

"It will not be."

"Down to ponies in the dining room. Apparently."

"That was not me," he said. "Let me make that very clear."

"Not wanting to take credit for your friend's idea?" A smile tugged at her lips, in spite of everything.

"Not wanting to take blame."

"She's very charming. And perhaps our... Perhaps our child will enjoy riding." Her eyes stung. "We get this chance. Not just to do this because it's right. But to give our child what we did not have."

"And that is?"

"Love."

"What is love to you?"

It was not a question she had expected him to ask. "You know," she said. "Love."

"I confess that I do not. I was never exposed to love as a child. Nor have I been exposed to it as an adult. At least, not in any way that I recognize." There was a cool detachment to his voice that was somehow more painful than a wrenching sob, and Eloise could only stare, stunned at the pain his admission created in her. Stunned at this easy admission of his own deficits. And even more, that he did not seem hurt by it. Only accepting. "On top of that, we have very different ideas of what love is presented throughout time in history. There is, of course, the modern concept of loving yourself before all others. There is romantic love. The love of a friend. There is the classic biblical interpretation. Love is patient.

Love is kind. It speaks more of a concept than anything specific. So what is it you mean when you say
*love*?"

She was taken aback by that absolutely, because
she found she did not have an answer. Because it
was only a feeling, and he wanted to know what it
looked like practically.

"I..."

"You say that you want our child to have love,
because as a society we're encouraged to talk about
love as though it is free and easy. As though every
parent loves their child, and every child their parent in return, but we know that is not the case, do
we not?"

"Yes."

"And then there is romantic love. Look at my parents' marriage. Is that love, do you think?"

"I do not think your father or my mother have ever
truly loved anyone."

"And yet, I imagine they would say they do.
Maybe they didn't think that they do. Because we
are conditioned to believe these feelings simply are.
That they are easy. That they are created inside of
us perhaps the same time as our physical hearts. But
what is love in a meaningful sense? In a way that
you can touch, and a way that you can taste and feel.
What is it? Because if it is not an action, then it does
not matter, does it? So when you speak of loving our
child, if you mean I will care for them, if you mean

I will offer support. Yes, I will. All of those things. Everything we did not get from our parents. In the same manner that I'm delivering your Christmas."

"But to you that isn't love?"

"I think perhaps love is a mass societal hallucination," he said, his voice grim. "If less people professed it as easily as they sneezed, then perhaps it might return to some original weight. Perhaps there would be something to understand. But I find myself cynical about the concept."

"Your mother loved you, surely."

He lifted a shoulder, and his gaze grew distant. "If she did, she never said. But my mother was the most stable influence in my life, that is certain. She saw to her duties, she inquired about my well-being. She was a good queen, and for all that my father offered her no recognition. Nothing but scorn."

She could hardly breathe after that scathing takedown of the entire institution of an emotion that she had believed to be the greatest thing in the entire world. Except... He had made it feel cracked. Crumbling. Was love and care the same thing? Duty and responsibility? Because when she thought of what she had been denied by her parents, those were the things that she would list. And yet it felt like there was more. Something self-sacrificial. Something self-sacrificial by choice.

"Would you have rather your mother said it?"

"Maybe at one time. But in the end of all things, it doesn't matter."

"You have a very grim view of the world."

"Is it? I don't think so. I think what is grim is how cheap words have become. We say them, we ask for them, we do not think about what they might mean. What they should mean. Perhaps if we did, people like our parents could not exist in such denial about their own behavior."

"Do you think they are in denial?"

"I hope so," he said. "Because if either of them has any real idea of the depth of their own depravity, if they realize how morally bankrupt they truly are and choose to walk that path anyway, I find that infinitely more upsetting."

"I suppose," she said. She felt chilled, all the way down to her soul.

She looked at him. And she felt like she understood something deeper about him than she had before.

She had wondered why. Why he wanted this child when he had been so dead set against the idea of children at all. Why he had come to get her. Why he wanted to marry her.

But she could see that he was actually a man of great depth and feeling, though ironically, after his previous statement about the awareness a person had of themselves, she knew that he did not see himself that way.

But he was a man who wished to intensely understand love before he ever professed it. And she realized, that was the cost of him.

She had escaped to that simple life, and nothing would ever be simple with Vincenzo. She let that sink in deep. Down through her skin, down into her blood. Her bones. Yes. Being with him would be a choice. A choice that would take her far away from where she had been before. From what she had known.

But perhaps she was ready now. Strong enough now. Perhaps she could be with him. She leaned in, across the small space of the dining table, and she pressed a kiss to his mouth.

He went still. And so did she. And it was like fire in her blood. Fire that joined in with that deep acceptance of the fact that there was no simplicity with a man like him.

And there never would be.

"I wish to go for a ride in the troika," she said.

"The pony cannot pull the troika," he said.

"Perhaps not. But we are in a winter wonderland. And you have promised me Christmas."

"I did. But I must call my friends first and tell them what manner of monster they have created."

"And what manner of monster is that?" she asked.

"Well, a kind very similar to them, I suppose."

"Tell me about your friends," she said.

"There isn't much to tell," he said, straightening. "We met at Oxford."

"I find that very interesting."

"What exactly?"

"Well, that you have friends. I wasn't trying to be mean when I said something about that. I don't really have friends. I have made casual acquaintances in the world of horticulture. Don't laugh. But I have never really known how to..." What she was about to say was dishonest in some ways. "I have struggled in my life to know how to connect to another person. Weirdly, my upbringing isn't very relatable."

It was one reason, she supposed, that it had been him from very early on.

"We are connected very much by similar pain," he said. "Each of them has their own... Difficulties. We are wealthy, powerful men, by any standards. And that made others in our sphere either seek to use us—which is foolish, because none of us would allow it—or it made them hate us. We found each other, and over the course of years confessed the great bleeding wounds our parents had left in us. You can have the entire world at your feet and still be missing a great many things."

She knew that to be true.

"If you want your troika ride, I suggest you get ready. I will have the staff prepare the horses in the stable. And I will have an outfit appropriate for the weather sent to you."

"Oh…"

"I think the word you're looking for is *thank you*."

"Yes," she said. "Thank you." And she suddenly felt foolish that she had kissed him. Because he had kissed her back, but it had been solicitous, not filled with heat.

But then, perhaps he was not attracted to her when she was like this. She was incredibly round. She could not blame him. She was surprised, honestly, that she was attracted to him still. She would've thought that her present condition excluded her from such feelings. How interesting that it did not. For she felt as if she would happily strip off all her clothes and climb into his lap, baby bump notwithstanding.

"I will meet you in an hour."

"All right."

# CHAPTER ELEVEN

In the end, Vincenzo decided to prepare the horses himself and did the rigorous task of getting them in the bridles on the troika. He would be sending Jag a picture of his middle finger later.

But it was a lovely sleigh, with intricate hand carvings on it and he knew that the gold leaf paint contained real gold, because Jag would never settle for anything less.

When Eloise appeared, it was like the sun coming out from behind the clouds. She was wearing a furry white hat, and a long white coat with fur around the edges. It went all the way down to the ground, sloping gently over her bump. There was a border of blue thread that ran from the collar all the way down to the floor.

She looked like a snow queen. Standing out there in the cold, her cheeks red, wisps of blond hair escaping the hat. When she had kissed him earlier, it had taken all of his strength not to clear the table and ravish her upon it. But he knew that he could not. He was trying to convince her to marry him, and ravishing her in her present state was not going to help with that. He had to show her that they had something that went beyond attraction. Attraction they knew they had. That was not up for debate. Attraction was what had gotten them into this situation in the first place. But she was asking for something else from him, and he was determined to give it. Determined to secure her acceptance of marriage.

His staff had packed a grand lunch in the sleigh, and they had placed thermoses of hot chocolate in the front. He wished that he'd asked them to add liquor to his own, but he had thought that it might be distasteful, considering Eloise's condition.

Still, he regretted it now.

"Oh," she said. "It's beautiful."

One of the horses shook their head, tossing their caramel-colored mane. And the harness jingled. There were, of course, bells upon the red leather straps.

"This is a Christmas fantasy," she said, her eyes jewel bright.

He had noticed that when they had flown on the private plane, she did not seem inured to excess. She had been raised in the palace, and yet, she did not seem to take luxury for granted. But perhaps that was because she had been kept adjacent to it, rather like an urchin with her nose pressed against the glass. For she might as well have been, as the use of it was denied to her.

It made him want to give her everything. Everything she had been denied.

"Leave it to Jag to go over-the-top."

"It's wonderful. I do rather wish Zeus's pony could lead the team."

"He will have to be content with being a stand-in in a live-action manger scene. That is perhaps more to his scale."

"Poor little thing. I'm afraid to ask why the pony. It seems as if it's some sort of inside joke."

"Zeus is under the impression that all women want a pony."

She laughed, the sound crystal like the snow all around them. "You know, I don't think he's wrong."

"He would tell you that he never is."

"And what do you think?"

"I think he is only wrong when he disagrees with me."

"I see."

Then they got into the troika, and there was a soft blanket inside, mottled gray and thick and plush. He draped it over her lap. And when she looked at him, her cheeks were crimson.

"Yes?"

"Nothing. No one has ever taken care of me before."

"Did you not ask for care? Is that not what a request for Christmas is?"

"I like it. But it occurs to me I have never really

taken care of anyone either. And I suppose I will be. Soon." She looked down at her stomach and placed her hand on the rounded bump there."

"I have never cared for anyone either."

"I don't think that's true," she said. "You have your friends. And it sounds to me like you've been there for each other when you've needed one another. I think that is quite commendable."

"I will accept any and all commendations as they come," he said.

"Naturally," she said.

He took his seat in the driver's spot and picked up the reins.

"It did not even occur to me to ask you if you knew how to drive it. Why would you know how to drive a Russian sleigh?"

"It is easy," he said, slapping the reins gently and urging the team forward.

These horses were soft mouthed and easily steered, the best. And the sleigh moved smoothly through the snow. They went away from the grounds of the palace, toward snow-dusted pines, going along the path that went through a thick canopy of trees.

She looked around, an expression of wonder on her face. "I half expect to see a lamppost."

He chuckled. "How about if I offered you some Turkish delight in exchange for betraying your entire family."

"You have essentially done that. But my family

was easy to betray." She sighed. "Turkish delight really isn't good enough to justify that sort of betrayal. Not if your family is good."

"Is that your firm stance?"

"Yes. I would need chocolate cake."

He chuckled. "Good to know."

"I am happy," she said quietly. "That your father has lost the throne. I am happy that my mother has lost her position here at the palace finally. I am... I am glad they were exposed. And I have to wonder what all that therapy was for if I can still take such pleasure in their downfall."

"I believe that is just called being human."

"It is an inconvenient thing. To be human. I think I tried really hard not to be."

"What do you mean?"

"Moving away the way that I did. Going off on my own, ensconcing myself in gardening and all of that. It was my very best attempt at not being vulnerable."

"You can hardly be blamed for wanting to avoid vulnerability."

"Maybe. But I wonder about all I have missed. And how... Well, how deeply in denial I am about my own human nature. I do not think I am half so benevolent as I let myself believe. When you and I met in the garden all those months ago, I told myself that I was going with you as a friend. But by the time I left your bed that morning, I knew. I knew that I was glorying in their destruction. And I was so judgmental of you. I felt above you. I felt better than you, but it was not fair."

"Do not be concerned about that. I feel better than most people."

She laughed. She couldn't help herself. She utterly howled. "I imagine you do." They lapsed into silence again, as the troika went deeper into the trees, the bells jingling.

"We shall take the baby out like this," she said, "for Christmas."

"Shall we?" he asked, his chest getting tight.

"Don't you think we ought to make some Christmas traditions?"

This was the first time she had really talked like she would stay.

"I don't know. Do you think they are important?"

"I do," she said.

"And how will we know?" he asked. "How will we know what matters?"

"Well," she said slowly. "I would think, we should try and remember everything that it felt like we were missing back when we were children. And make sure our child does not miss that?"

"A long list," he said.

And he suddenly wondered if he had never wanted a child because he wanted to end his line, or if he had known that...

That it would be difficult for a man who had never experienced having a real father.

A father who cared.

He wanted to be the right kind of father.

And he had no real idea what that meant.

Right then, he made a decision to show her something he had never shown another person. As the road forked, he went to the left, and it narrowed and went windy, and the ground became thicker with snow as they exited the trees.

"Where are we going?"

"You'll see."

They rounded a curve, and the mountains in front of them disappeared. And about twenty feet ahead, so did the snow.

"Vincenzo," she said, putting her hand on his thigh.

"No worries."

He stopped the team of horses, just at the edge of a ravine that overlooked a crystal lake, frozen over with ice, the sun sparkling over the surface.

"Vincenzo…"

"It's beautiful," he said. "Is it not?"

"Yes. What is this place?"

"I used to come here as a boy. It is part of the unspoiled wilderness in Arista. As far as I know, there is no path to get down to the lake, though I thought as a boy of many different methods to try and get there. I wanted to be part of the wilderness. Most of all, I wanted to escape the oppression of the palace. And so I used to come here. And I used to sit. And I used to think of escape. But there was no way to escape. Not from where I was. It was then that I had to accept that…in the end of all things, I had to turn back and confront the evil in my world. I could not simply run away into the wilderness. There was no path."

"That must've been terrifying to realize as a child."

"Did I ever tell you when I realized that my father was bad?"

"No," she said.

He had never told anyone this story. Not even Rafael, Jag and Zeus.

"When the antiliquor laws in Arista went into effect, I remember seeing my father drink a glass of wine with dinner every night. And when I tried to question him about it, he said that some men made the rules, and others had to live by them. And I knew it was wrong. Down in my soul, I knew it was wrong. That one life should be lived here in the palace, while another would be lived among the people. I knew that his control was simply for the sake of control, and not out of conviction. And at first, like I said, I wanted to run. But I realized someone had to fix it. Someone had to. And the longer things went on, I only saw more contradictions between the rules my father made in the edicts he issued and the way that he lived. And no one did anything to stop him. No one spoke against him. I realized that person would have to be me."

She nodded slowly. "What a terrible realization."

"It was a powerful realization, and I am glad for it. You cannot wait for others to do the right thing. It is up to us. Each of us. We cannot claim something is not our problem. If it exists in the world, it is a problem for all of us."

"You are a very good man. You cover it quite skillfully with hardness. But you are a warrior."

He did not know what to say to that, so he simply looked out at the view. He felt like a warrior at times. But rather than wearing armor, his whole body was covered over in a protective layer. Calcified. He looked at her, and he felt drawn to her. Pulled toward her like there was a magnet between them. Something he could not deny.

But she had wanted a nice outing; she did not ask to be ravished. Again, he would have to practice self-control. Damned inconvenient when he wanted to do anything but. "We should go back."

"We haven't even had a hot chocolate."

"I do not wish you to catch too much of a cold."

"I'm fine. I'm pregnant. I'm not broken."

*Pregnant.* With his child. They really were standing on the brink of everything changing.

But it was not that escape he dreamed of as a boy. And it wasn't that simple life she had talked about either. It was something else. Something he couldn't say that he understood.

"The doctor said you were healthy?"

She nodded. "Yes. I had my standard checkups and…"

"Are you due another one?"

"Soon. But I'm not concerned."

"Good to hear."

"Women have been doing this for a very long time."

"Yes," he said. "But it is not always safe."

"But there's no reason to believe that mine will not be."

Suddenly, his chest went tight, clutched with something unfamiliar. He could not figure out what it was. He had never experienced anything like it before in his life. He had the sudden urge to grab her and gather her up close to his chest. And all around him the world seemed precarious. The trees laden with snow that might tip from the weight of it. The precipice in front of them, and the lake down below. All of these sights that he had wanted to show her suddenly seemed like they might rebel against them both. He was aware of how fragile she looked. In all that white.

He had been prepared to seduce her, to entice her into his plan of vengeance. He had made love to her that night months ago with both of them burning white-hot from battle, the thrill of victory.

And now it was his own need. A great, ravenous beast that burned in him like a monster he feared could consume them both.

But she was pregnant with his child. He could not touch her like this.

"Let's go," he said.

The farther away they got from the precipice, the more the feeling faded. But he only wished that he could understand what had started it in the first place.

Or perhaps, he did not.

# CHAPTER TWELVE

ELOISE COULDN'T UNDERSTAND. Vincenzo had been so sweet to her today. And it was weird. Because he was many things, but he was hardly sweet, and he was being solicitous in a way that... It seemed odd. She had kissed him this morning, and he had not done anything to follow up on it.

She paced back and forth in her room, wearing a soft, gauzy white nightgown that made her feel elegant, or rather like a cloud. A round, fluffy cloud. Perhaps she simply didn't appeal to him. He had been sweet to her on the trip in the troika. And he had shown her the view of the water and she felt... In many ways she felt closer to him than she ever had. But she missed the heat. She missed the fire. And she hoped that this was not the compromise that had to occur. That in order for them to have conversations. In order for them to connect, in order for them not to be bogged down in misunderstandings and recriminations, they had to be... Friends.

Not that there was anything bad about being

friends. But she wanted the fire. He had always felt like more to her than that. A connection that had come from nowhere. A connection that had taken root deep inside of her chest. He had never been anything quite so bland as a friend, and she did not wish him to be now.

She remembered the wildness between them, that moment when they had been rejoicing in their accomplishments. In taking down his father.

She was remorseful about that emotion, but there was something about the dark edge of that experience that had affected her. That had made her feel... Wild.

Did she have to be glorying in something so dark in order to experience that kind of explosion of passion? In order to create it in someone else?

Without thinking, she exited the bedroom. She began to walk down the hallway, her throat dry. Her heart was thundering in her chest.

She already knew what she was doing without it even forming in her mind as a coherent thought. She wanted him. And she wanted to be brave.

She was trying to find a way to join up these pieces of herself. This girl who loved planting, who wanted a Christmas and who wanted birthday parties. Who wanted these soft, simple things. And who felt the dark turn to light when her enemies were slain, and who wanted to tear Vincenzo's clothes off and wanted him to do the same to her.

Who had gloried in the animalistic need between them, and who had sat in the troika watching the falling snow all around them. Who had enjoyed the silence and that lake view.

Because it was all inside of her. All the same, but right now it felt distinct. Separate. She had been certain that he had chosen a path and she had chosen another and those paths could not meet.

But they could. They did. She had the feeling they met at that cliff side. Tranquil beauty and a sense of danger.

But she could not quite figure out how to make sense of it. That's what she was searching for now.

She had the sense that he would not be in his room. She knew where his study was in the palace. Where his father's had been before him. It was funny to wander around the palace now, this place that had always been filled with dark foreboding, but now was covered in icicles and lights. All for her. And he didn't understand it, but he had done it anyway, and surely there must be something of emotion in that.

*Or he's just trying to manipulate you.*

What was manipulation? And what was caring? Did either of them even know the difference?

Her heart was pounding in her head now. Making it difficult to breathe. She pushed open the door to his study and found him there, sitting at the desk. There was a fire in the grand fireplace, and she could see snow falling outside the window in the darkness.

"What are you doing here?" he asked.

"I came looking for you." She walked toward him.

"Is everything all right?"

"Everything is fine. It's just… It's just that… Am I repulsive to you now?"

"What?"

"Me. In this…" She swished her nightgown around. "In this shape. Do you not want me?"

He stared at her from the desk, the firelight illuminating the hollows of his face. His eyes looked black. Like coal.

"Is that what you think?"

"Yes. I kissed you."

"You did. And asked me to take you on a sleigh ride."

"And you did not try to kiss me."

"No. But you did not ask me to. You asked me for a ride in the troika."

"And you gave it to me. And I appreciate it. But I did expect you to try and…"

"I thought that you wanted me to give you Christmas."

"I want both. I want Christmas, and I want you to look at me as if you want to devour me. I want conversation, but I also want you to kiss me."

"A kiss… Eloise, I could not stop at just a kiss."

"You couldn't?"

He stood and rounded the desk slowly, his mannerisms that of a prowling cat. "Eloise," he said, his voice frayed. "It is a torture to be so near you and not touch you. To see your body so luscious and round with the evidence that you carry my child, and to keep my hands off you. I have wanted nothing more than to grab hold of you and crush you to my body from the moment I first saw you standing in your house. But I have been restrained, because I did not want to put you under undue stress. And I have commanded that you marry me. And I am... I am at your mercy," he said, the words splintering like thin ice. "I would not wish to do something to distress you, for fear that you would refuse me."

"You're afraid that I will refuse you?"

"Of course I am. You have not agreed to be my wife. You have not agreed to be mine, and it all hangs by a thread. This balance is... It is precarious." He dropped to his knees before her, and she startled. Then his thumb was at her ankle, massaging her there. And he continued up, sweeping the nightgown up her thighs, past her hips, and pulling it over her head, leaving her completely nude in the firelight. And she felt... She felt beautiful. The way he looked at her, the way the fire glowed across her curves. He made her feel like a goddess.

"*Diana,*" he said.

And it made her feel warm all over, because she knew that he was thinking the same that she had been. A goddess.

"Goddess of the hunt. But it is I who would have been in pursuit of you."

"I'm the one that came to your study," she said, her breath a whisper.

"Perhaps… Perhaps we hunt for each other."

"Perhaps," she said, the words coming out soft as a feather.

He stood away from her, unbuttoned his shirt slowly, his body bathed in an orange glow. The dips and hollows of his body highlighted by the harsh flame. He removed all his clothes, and he looked like a god himself. Or perhaps simply… A predator. Like he had said. Perhaps they both hunted one another. Then he moved to her and kissed her. But this was not tentative. Not the polite kiss between two people seated at the dining table, where others could walk in at any moment. It was deep and hard, carnal. It held in it the promise of everything he had just said. It made his words into truth, as he devoured her mouth, licking deep and stealing her breath away. He kissed her neck and then moved down to her breasts. He cupped her, squeezing them, drawing his thumbs over her nipples. "Beautiful," he rasped. "I love your curves. You were concerned, about your roundness, even before you carried the baby. I find you lush. Feminine. Exquisite. And this new shape… It is unbearable. I cannot breathe for how exquisite you are."

She moaned as he lowered his head, drawing one

tightened bud between his lips and sucking hard. She was so sensitive there now, she felt it all echo between her legs. Felt her desire for him erupt like sparks. She was very nearly there, just from the attention to her breast. He sank lower, trailing a line of kisses over her rounded bump. And she felt the baby shift inside her. He stopped and looked up at her, his expression fierce. "Was that?"

"Yes," she said, softly. "The baby moves."

He got to his feet and pressed his palm against her stomach. "It moves?"

"Yes," she said.

He caught her gaze and held it there for a long moment. And something swelled inside her chest, and she was sure looking into his eyes the same thing was in him. And she wanted to tell him. Wanted to say it.

Because this was love. It was pure, and it was real. And it was more than a responsibility. It was more than an attachment. It was a miracle. A miracle that defied explanation. "It is incredible," he said.

"I know," she said.

He kissed her hungrily then, breaking the softness of the moment, driving her back and then guiding her gently down into a chair. Then he knelt down before her and spread her legs, lifting her thighs up over his shoulder and tasting her as he had done the first time they were together. She gasped, arching into him, enjoying his loss of control. But it was the combination of this moment and the moment just prior that sent her over the edge. That fierceness in his face. The realization that this was real. Everything.

She sobbed out her pleasure, and he rose up from the floor, picking her up off the chair and wrapping her thighs around his body, before seating them both again. Then he thrust up inside her, and she let her head fall back. He gripped her hips, driving up into her, his eyes wild. And she lost herself.

Because here it was. The sweetness combined with the passion. Need combined with want too.

The simplicity of creation, of life and the dark broken pieces of their desire for one another. It filled her. Consumed her. Changed her. This man, who was the father of her child, her future husband, her lover.

He was everything, just as she was.

He was a warrior, a protector. He could touch her gently and with passion.

And when her desire broke over her, it burst behind her eyelids with every color under the sun, bright and brilliant, sweet and pastel, dark and rich, and for the first time she understood what it was to be Eloise. Not Eloise ignored. Not Eloise hidden. But Eloise, fully in charge of herself. In command of her desires. Then he cried out his own release, and their eyes met. And right then, she felt whole.

He rested his head against her neck and whispered, "I smell roses."

She didn't know what it meant. But it felt like a

declaration. "Vincenzo," she whispered. "I'll marry you."

He looked up at her, the intensity in his gaze burning hotter than the fire. "You'll marry me?"

"Yes."

"We will marry on Christmas Eve."

"Yes."

He gripped her chin, holding it tight. "Say it again."

"Yes," she said again.

# CHAPTER THIRTEEN

"WE ARE GETTING married on Christmas Eve," he said, speaking to his friends through the computer screen.

"What a shock—Vincenzo Moretti's had his way," Jag said.

"It was the stock options," Rafael said.

"I think we all know it was the pony."

"It was the troika," Vincenzo said.

"Is that what the kids are calling it these days?" Zeus quipped.

"I expect you all to be there."

"Absolutely. I would not stay away from court if you were being sentenced to life in prison," Jag said. "I will certainly not miss your marriage."

"Nice," Zeus said.

"You're doing the right thing," Rafael said. "It is right that you marry the mother of your child."

"Do you always do what is right, Rafael?" Zeus asked, his tone dry.

"Yes. Do you not?"

"I think you know I avoid it at all costs whenever possible."

"Not me. Honor is everything. It is all a man has," Rafael responded.

"Well," Zeus said. "We all have thrones. You do not. At least not permanently."

"It may shock you to learn I don't care," Rafael returned.

"Enough of this," Vincenzo said. "You must all come, and you must all be kind to her."

"Of course we'll be kind to her," Jag said.

"*You* are another matter," Zeus finished.

"Friendship is overrated," Vincenzo said. But he did not think that was true. Friendship had been the only good thing in his life. The friendship with these men. But then there was Eloise. The memory of last night made him burn. Eloise was perfect. Brilliant. She had been exquisite in the firelight. All glowing curves and pleasure.

"We will see you Christmas Eve," Zeus said.

"See you Christmas Eve." He rang off the call and paced the length of the room. There were only three days until the wedding. And he intended it to be a massive celebration. He would make a wedding so bright and brilliant that Eloise would be radiant with it. And he found that drove him most of all. Something had changed inside him that night all those months ago. He had begun to want things, not for himself, not for the greater good, but for her. When he was in her arms, what seemed faint became all the more clear. As if the intangible suddenly made sense in a way it never had before.

It was a feeling that rested somewhere next to the fear he had felt when he was out in the troika with her. But it was something different. Something more. And when he had put his hand on her stomach and felt the baby moving…

It had made everything all the more real. That was certain.

He left his study and went down to the dining room, where she was already sitting, chatting with the housekeeper. The smile on her face made him stop where he stood. She was radiant. But there was something more. There was something to the light in her expression. Something bright in her eyes. And he could not fully fathom what it was. Only that it immobilized him. Utterly. Completely. He didn't think he had ever seen anyone look quite so happy in this palace.

Perhaps it would be all right.

"All plans are going forward for the wedding," he said, moving deeper into the room.

"Oh, good," she said. "A Christmas Eve wedding really is so exciting."

She beamed. The smile quite unlike anything he had ever seen before. She was beautiful.

One of his staff came in then, holding an envelope. "A message for you," he said, addressing Eloise.

"Oh," she said. "Thank you."

She took the envelope from his hand and opened it. As she began to read, her expression fell. It was like a light had been extinguished, and it made his chest seize up.

"What is it?"

"It's nothing," she said, holding the letter close to her chest.

"It is something," he said. He held his hand out, the demand obvious. She gave in, placing the paper in his palm.

He looked down at the letter. And his blood turned to ice.

Congratulations on whoring yourself out to royalty. Do you honestly think you're any different from me? You're smart, though. You're carrying the heir. But all your principles, and his, look foolish. You are no different. Just remember that.

It was from her mother.

"That snake," he said.

"She's not wrong. Except... She's all wrong." She looked up at him, but her expression was sad now, and he hated her mother for that.

"Explain."

"It's not the same between us as it was between her and my father. And I am not carrying this child to get your money. You know that."

He did. Because she had been happy to hide the baby away from him. He did not suspect Eloise of being at all like her mother. But still it was a terrible thing, to watch that haunted look in her eyes. Because no matter what she said, she felt the pain from this letter very deeply. It didn't matter that she shouldn't. It didn't matter that she knew she wasn't her mother. She felt it.

And he felt a burden of responsibility for causing this pain.

"Is it bad?" he asked. "Being here?"

"I'm not going to pretend it's my favorite."

"Of course not," he said.

"But… Where else would I be?"

He gritted his teeth together. "Yes. Where else…"

But in his mind's eye, he saw her back in her garden. Surrounded by her flowers.

That was where she would be.

If not for him. If not for this.

She had been brave, a warrior in all of this, but she had not chosen this path in the beginning. He had. Or rather he had been put on it in a way that felt fated. Unavoidable.

But she wanted love.

And he did not know what it was.

The evils of the past would always be there. This letter proved it.

He had dragged her back into hell along with him, and he did not know what to make of that revelation.

"I am taking dinner in my study tonight. I hope you enjoy your meal."

Then he turned and left her there, feeling like a coward. Feeling ineffective. Feeling like…

He felt like an ass. And he was.

But there was nothing to be done about it.

# CHAPTER FOURTEEN

HE HAD BEEN distant for two days. And now it was the eve of their wedding, and she didn't understand. She didn't understand why this man, who had taken her out and showed her his favorite view, something he had never shown anyone before, was suddenly like a stone again.

Because she and Vincenzo had nearly become friends, and then after the way they had made love by the fire, it had all become more. And she just couldn't credit what had happened because of this distance between them. It was disturbing and upsetting. And she wished… She wished that she knew exactly how to reach him.

*What is love?*

She had been thinking so much about that statement. And she knew the answer, but she didn't know how to tell him. That was the problem. Because she knew that she loved him. And she knew that she loved their child. And that he did too. She had seen it in his eyes when he had felt that miracle. But how…

*You have to tell him.*

But it scared her. The idea of telling him. Because she had tried… It reminded her of being eighteen. Of trying to forge that connection between them that he had not felt at the time. It reminded her of that humiliation. Of that sadness. And she didn't want to experience it again.

But what other choice was there?

She had had a moment of wholeness. Of being Eloise as she was intended to be. Rather than Eloise, fragmented by the life she had been given. But she would live her entire life in fragments, only experiencing that blinding, wonderful feeling of being complete when he was inside her. When she had a feeling that she might be able to experience it all the time. Yes. She might.

And wasn't that worth it? Wasn't that worth the risk?

It was only her feelings, after all. And whatever happened with those, she could survive them. It was only feelings.

She had a doctor's appointment today, and he was going to accompany her. She had been wanting to leave the gender of the child a surprise, but having a scan done this late in the game might reveal everything.

But it would be okay if he… She wondered if he would connect even more, having seen the child. Knowing if it was a son or a daughter.

Those thoughts were all swirling around in her head when the doctor arrived at her bedroom.

How different it was to be treated when one was going to be a queen. The doctor was followed closely by Vincenzo, who appeared in a cloud of ferocity and intensity. As he was wont to do.

But this seemed even more pronounced than usual.

"Good afternoon," the doctor said. "It is an honor to treat you today."

"Oh," she said, feeling her cheeks heat. "Thank you."

"Let us get this started," Vincenzo said.

She readied herself, lay on the bed and waited.

The doctor shifted her nightgown, pushing it up over her bump. Then put a warmed gel on her skin, gliding the Doppler over the top of it.

And then the sound of the baby's heartbeat filled the screen, and she saw the silhouette of their head. An arm pressed right up by their face.

"Vincenzo," she whispered.

She hadn't seen the baby in a few months, and it was incredible how much more like a baby it looked.

"Oh, Vincenzo."

She heard Vincenzo draw close to the bed, and then felt him as he dropped to his knees beside it. She looked at him, at the way his dark eyes were rapt on the screen. The doctor was moving over various parts now, the baby's belly, legs, feet. Then back up to the head, where they could see the profile.

Vincenzo said nothing. His face was simply set in stone, caught somewhere between terror and awe. She understood. She felt that way too. "This is it," she whispered. "Vincenzo. This is it."

And she knew that he understood what she meant. This was love. It was as certain as she could ever be that he would understand. Because she could see it. She could see it in his eyes. And she felt it reflected inside her. This terrifying, momentous, wondrous thing.

"And do you want to know the gender?" The doctor asked.

"No," Vincenzo said. "No."

But there was something strange in his voice that she could not quite understand.

The doctor finished the exam, and then Vincenzo turned to leave at the same time as the doctor. "Stay with me," she said.

He stopped.

Skerret chose that moment to come out from under the bed and jump up onto the mattress. Investigating the extra person in the room, not brave enough exactly to take on two. The little gray creature was no less mangy now in looks than she had been when Eloise had first adopted her. She would always look like a ditch cat. There was no getting around it.

"I think Skerret is requesting your affection," she said, feeling mildly amused when she jumped down from the bed and wove between Vincenzo's legs.

"Skerret will have to be disappointed on that score."

"She's not afraid of disappointment. In fact, I think she's quite inured to it. She'll wear you down eventually."

She felt for a moment like she was actually talking about herself.

"And how have you been? Since your mother's letter?"

She frowned. "Oh. It's not unexpected. She's spiteful. It has nothing to do with us. Nothing to do with where we are going."

"I do not think we should get married."

"What?" she asked, feeling as if she'd been struck, the pain of those words a physical blow.

"I do not think we should get married. I think you should go back to Virginia." His words were hard, and so was his face.

She felt as if the bottom had dropped out of the world.

"Are you... Angry at me?" It was all she could think. That she had done something wrong. Again. He had sent her away once before with offers of money because he believed the worst of her. Had something happened again?

"Vincenzo," she said, a pleading note in her voice.

"What is it? You know I am… You know I care for you…"

"It is not you," he said. "But this place… There is poison in these walls. And no amount of Christmas lights is ever going to make it different. You deserve better than this. Our child deserves better than this."

"Better than being the heir to a throne? Better than this country?" Tears filled her eyes. "Better than having his father?"

"I will still be his father. But if we do not marry, then he is not the heir. If we do not marry, then… All will go according to plan on my end, and you will not have to spend your life trapped here."

"Did I say that I was trapped?"

"No. You didn't. But I see it. I see it even if you do not."

"You… You utter bastard. I did not ask you for this." Anger boiled over inside her. He was talking about walls, but the only wall here was him. He was so hard. And he would not tell her the truth. He was shut down and merciless in his coldness, and what was she supposed to do with that? "How… How can you do this? After you've just seen our child?"

"This why I have to do this. It is why I have to."

"I love you," she said. "I love you, Vincenzo, and I didn't tell you this before because you want to know things about this feeling that I don't think I can answer. Because it is something in my blood. Something that feels as much a part of me as anything else that I am. And I cannot come up with a way to explain. I cannot think of how I might define it. I know that you want that. But I can only tell you what I feel. In my heart. And it is love for you. A love that has been there for… Well more than ten years. I love you. The more that I get to know you, the more that I feel it. And it is more than simply wanting to take care of you. Wanting to protect you. Wanting to sleep with you. I am carrying a piece of you inside of me. This evidence of the passion between us…"

"Yes," he said, "and I am the result of my mother and father's union. But there was no love between them. What of your father? You've never even met him. That is not evidence of love, Eloise. It is simply an aftereffect of sex."

"But the child…"

"I don't feel it," he said. "I don't feel it. You said this was it. And if I cannot… I refuse to have our child grow up as we did. I refuse it."

He didn't feel it. He didn't feel it even for their child.

"Maybe it is because I never saw it," he said. "Never heard it."

"Neither did I. But I still know enough to understand it when I am fortunate enough to have it. Why can't you?"

"Perhaps I'm just broken, more so than you."

"Your friends," she said. "Do you not love them?"

"It's different."

"It's not. It all comes from here." She pressed her hand to his chest. "It all comes from here. From who you are. And I cannot... How can you think that there isn't love there?"

"I will send you back to Virginia."

"No," she said.

"I am sending you back."

"You can't."

"Then you will live here as you did as a child. Ignored. Unwanted. Is that what you would like?"

She drew back, feeling as if he had struck her. He might as well have.

"Vincenzo..."

"I will ready the plane immediately."

"Vincenzo!" She screamed his name, because he would not yell. She unleashed her fury because he had closed everything inside of him.

And he stood there, his breath coming hard, his chest heaving with it. "It is not this place that is poison, Eloise. It is me. It is my blood. And I will not poison us all."

And that was how she found herself bundled onto a private plane, numb. Crying. She had no recollection of the flight. None at all. She was just suddenly standing in front of her door in Virginia with the snow falling softly behind her, and her cat carrier in hand.

She walked inside and looked into the corner where her Christmas tree had been. She realized it was still at the palace. And for some reason it was that, that stupid thing, that made her burst into tears. That made it all feel like too much. For some reason, it was the tree that pushed it beyond the pale. She began to weep. Like her heart was broken. Because it was. Because she no longer had Vincenzo, and nothing would ever be right again.

*You have your child.*

Yes, she did. And her simple life. Except Eloise was not simple. Not anymore, and perhaps she never had been. Eloise had learned to want it all.

And taking half felt unacceptable.

He did not expect his friends to show up early. But they did.

And he was drunk.

"What the hell is this?" Zeus asked.

"Nothing," he said, straightening at his desk, feeling worse for wear.

"Liar," Rafael said. "You look like hell. And you smell worse."

"I find you offensive in every way," Jag said. "Where is your woman?"

"She is not my woman," he said.

"Then something's changed," Rafael said.

"Nothing has changed. I simply realized that I was allowing her to live through what we had already endured as children. It was not right. I sent her home."

"You did what?" Jag asked. "You sent your pregnant fiancée home the day before your wedding?"

"It had to be done."

"Did it?" he asked. "I do not believe you."

"I didn't ask for your belief, friend. I, in fact asked for nothing. Least of all for the three of you to be standing in my study."

"Too bad for you," Zeus said. "This is what friends are for. Get yourself together."

"I'm together. I am doing the right thing."

"You're not doing the right thing. You're doing the easy thing," Rafael said. "You saw her struggling, and rather than doing something to fix it, you sent her where you didn't have to look at it. Rather than doing the work to figure out exactly how you needed to change this place so that it was not the same place that you grew up in, you removed her. And you're going to what? Sink away in your misery?"

"How dare any of you lecture me on feelings."

"You do not have any, you are a coward. Not a King."

"And you are in my palace."

"How quickly he has come to view it as his palace," Jag said. "For all his talk of not even wanting the throne."

"What would you have me do? You'd have me keep a woman with me who professes to love me when I cannot offer her the same in return?"

Zeus lifted a brow. "I am hardly one to advocate

for the institution of marriage, or love. But I can hardly see why you're standing there acting as if the woman carrying your child being in love with you is some conundrum you cannot get past."

"Because of her happiness. It is for her."

"Or is it for your own protection?"

Vincenzo didn't want to speak to them anymore. Instead, he strode out of the study and down the stairs, and before he knew what he was doing, he was walking. In the snow. Walking until he reached that spot on the hill that overlooked the lake. The wind whipped up furiously around him, his coat blowing around his knees. He stared into the snowflakes, which burned holes through his skin with the freezing cold.

But he didn't care. "Eloise," he said.

*This is it.*

He could not understand what she meant. He couldn't.

Because all he felt was pain. The same pain that had been in his chest from the time he was a boy. When he looked at his mother and saw her sad. When he looked at his father and found him lacking. When he felt lonely. When he had been isolated as a boy. This feeling was...

He thought of his mother again, and a great pain burst in his chest.

*This is it.*

He recognized this feeling as grief. Not as love. And then he saw his mother's face.

*I love you.*

The words exited his mouth before he could even think them through.

He looked at his mother, and that was what he thought.

But it was painful. It was not a glory.

*No one has ever said it to me.*

No one except for Eloise.

And then, even in the midst of the snow, it was like he could smell roses.

And he knew.

It wasn't the simple life that called to him. And it wasn't a rose petal on the wind.

It was Eloise. And loving her.

Love had been grief for all his life because there had been no one there to return it. And when he had looked upon his own child, he had felt that same pain because he felt ill-equipped to deal with it.

But Eloise was right. It was love. And it was something more than he had ever imagined it could be. Because pain was part of it. And perhaps this was why people did not love in this way. Unless they couldn't help it.

Unless they had to.

*He loved her.*

He loved her. He loved their baby.

He had loved all along. He had loved his mother,

who had never said it to him as she wallowed in her own grief. He had loved his father, even while knowing the man was flawed.

Love had always been inside him.

And now, it finally had a chance to take a shape other than this pain.

If only Eloise did not hate him.

He hoped that she didn't. To have come this far, only to lose love again would be unbearable.

He walked back to the palace, completely unaware of the cold now. "We must go," he said to his friends. "To Virginia."

"Really?" Zeus asked. "That's so surprising. You had a change of heart after your isolated self-flagellation walk."

"Shut your mouth for once and gather up as many Christmas decorations as you can. And we must make sure to get her wedding dress."

# CHAPTER FIFTEEN

SHE HAD NOT put up a new Christmas tree, and she was slightly regretful. There was no reason to compound her misery, after all. And yet part of her wished to. Wished to wallow in it. In the pain of not having him with her.

*Vincenzo.*

She loved him. The fact that he had done this to her didn't change that.

It was Christmas Eve, and she was miserable.

Skerret was sitting by the fire in the sweater that she had knitted for her, looking as fine as a ditch cat could.

"At least one of us is content."

The cat said nothing. She only stared back with contemptuous yellow eyes.

Then suddenly there was a knock on the door, and she had a terrible flash of the two other times this had occurred. But twice was perhaps possible, three times, after he had so soundly rejected her, was not. But who else would be at the door on Christmas Eve?

She scrambled out of her chair and waddled to the door.

And when she opened it, it was not just Vincenzo standing there, wearing a dark suit, but three other men, just as tall and imposing, and all so handsome it was stunning.

These men had to be his friends. They had all gone to school together. How had the women on campus gotten anything done?

"Oh," she said.

"She's beautiful," one of the men said.

"Luminous," another said, walking in past her.

"A goddess," said the third. And then suddenly all but Vincenzo were in her house.

"Agreed," Vincenzo said. "I have brought your wedding dress. Because I would still very much like to marry you."

She blinked, then took a step out of the house, closing the front door behind her and isolating them. "What?"

"I realized something. I realized that I love you. Because I found an answer to my question. I was wrong. Love is something born into all of us. What I think we learn is how to suppress it in favor of self-ishness. What I think we learn is to ignore it when it hurts too much. And so, for me, all love was pain. When I looked at our baby, all I saw was grief, and when you told me you loved me, all I felt was loneliness. Because that is all I have ever known when it comes to love."

"Oh, Vincenzo."

"You do not need to pity me. For I was a fool. And I hurt you. I regret that. Bitterly."

"But…"

"But I'm here. I'm here because I love you. I'm here because I want you. I've never said those words to anyone. I have never realized that feeling before now. And I hope that is enough. I hope that it is clear that what I say is true."

"Even if I didn't believe you, I wouldn't be strong enough to tell you no." She flung her arms around his neck and kissed him. "Because I love you. I was willing to love you through you figuring out what love was. I didn't need to hear it back right away."

"I know," he said. "But I was just so… I cannot explain." He shook his head. "Except that I was terrified. And I hated admitting that. More than anything."

"I'm sure."

"Zeus is ordained. And he is ready to perform the wedding now. I'm ready to marry you now."

She blinked back tears. "That's good. Because I'm ready too."

From behind the garment bag he pulled a bouquet of roses and extended it to her. "When you told me about your simple life, I could feel the longing for it in a fleeting way. The scent of roses on the wind.

But I realized today it was deeper than that. It was my longing for you. Not simplicity. But simply to be where you are. And I got these roses because, for me, it is that intangible thing made real."

She put on her dress, floaty and ethereal, skimming over her bump, and clutched her roses to her chest, looking at herself in the mirror and feeling... Whole.

They were all out in the garden. In the snow. And as she and Vincenzo exchanged vows, just them and Vincenzo's closest friends, she felt she understood love in the truest, most complete way possible.

"I now pronounce you husband and wife. King and Queen."

"You cannot pronounce me King," Vincenzo said. "There is to be a coronation."

"I can pronounce you whatever I like," Zeus said. "I'm officiating."

And with that, they kissed. And it didn't matter what they were called. It didn't matter if the monarchy was abolished or not. It didn't matter if they lived in this cottage in Virginia, or in the palace. They were each other's home. And that was all that mattered.

The coronation was met with great enthusiasm by the people of Arista. Jag and Zeus were in attendance, but not Rafael, who had the wedding of his brother to see to. And it was shocking when they heard the news later. That the wedding had not in fact gone on as intended. But the bride had been taken—by Rafael himself!

"Now that was unexpected," Zeus said.

"Entirely," Jag said. "He never breaks the rules. Or does anything half so interesting as kidnapping women."

"There is a story there," Zeus said. "And I am going to get it."

Eloise thought that she had been filled up with love, more than she could ever hold inside of herself, with her husband, his friends, the people of Arista. But when their son, Mauro Moretti was born, they knew different. Both of them. And they found that the miraculous thing about love was the way that it expanded. To fit everything. The way that it colored every breath, the way that it informed absolutely everything.

After much restructuring, and a vote, it was decided that Arista would retain the monarchy, at least as stabilizing figureheads. And the people were happy to welcome Vincenzo as their King, and Mauro as the next. Especially with more freedom to choose the laws of the land and the knowledge that their leader was just. And that his son would be raised in the same way.

That summer, they went back to Virginia. And spent time in the garden where Vincenzo had first found her.

She had planted roses. Everywhere. For they would always be that concrete symbol of their love. And much to her surprise, with the baby strapped to his chest, Vincenzo rolled up his sleeves and knelt in the dirt beside her, digging a hole with his hands for the new rosebush she had bought.

"I never thought I would see King Vincenzo Moretti on his knees in the dirt, much less beside me."

"And I never thought I would be loved. Yet now I find myself overfilled with it. And I've never been so happy."

"Neither have I, Vincenzo. Neither have I."

There were no sad places left in the world for them. No dark, deep hollows of loneliness. For their love filled them up.

Eloise had wanted a simple life. And in some way she supposed she had one.

Simply perfect.

She started humming.

\* \* \* \* \*

*Blown away by*
Crowned for His Christmas Baby?
*Look out for the next instalments in
the Pregnant Princesses quartet,
coming soon from Jackie Ashenden, Caitlin Crews
and Marcella Bell!*

*In the meantime, why not get lost in these other
Maisey Yates stories?*

His Forbidden Pregnant Princess
The Queen's Baby Scandal
Crowning His Convenient Princess
Crowned for My Royal Baby
A Bride for the Lost King

*Available now!*

# WE HOPE YOU ENJOYED
## THIS BOOK FROM

*Escape to exotic locations where passion knows no bounds.*

Welcome to the glamorous lives of royals and billionaires, where passion knows no bounds. Be swept into a world of luxury, wealth and exotic locations.

**8 NEW BOOKS AVAILABLE EVERY MONTH!**

### #3969 CINDERELLA'S BABY CONFESSION
by Julia James

Alys's unexpected letter confessing to the consequences of their one unforgettable night has ironhearted Nikos reconsidering his priorities. He'll bring Alys to his Greek villa, where he *will* claim his heir. By first unraveling the truth...and then her!

### #3970 PREGNANT BY THE WRONG PRINCE
*Pregnant Princesses*
by Jackie Ashenden

Molded to be the perfect queen, Lia's sole rebellion was her night in Prince Rafael's powerful arms. She never dared dream of more. But now Rafael's stopping her arranged wedding—to claim her and the secret she carries!

### #3971 STRANDED WITH HER GREEK HUSBAND
by Michelle Smart

Marooned on a Greek island with her estranged but gloriously attractive husband, Keren has nowhere to run. Not just from the tragedy that broke her and Yannis apart, but from the joy and passion she's tried—and failed—to forget...

### #3972 RETURNING FOR HIS UNKNOWN SON
by Tara Pammi

Eight years after a plane crash left Christian with no memory of his convenient vows to Priya, he returns—and learns of his heir! To claim his family, he makes Priya an electrifying proposal: three months of living together...as man and wife.

### #3973 ONE SNOWBOUND NEW YEAR'S NIGHT
by Dani Collins

Rebecca has one New Year's resolution: divorce Donovan Scott. Being snowbound at his mountain mansion isn't part of the plan. And what happens when it becomes clear the chemistry that led to their elopement is still very much alive?

### #3974 VOWS ON THE VIRGIN'S TERMS
*The Cinderella Sisters*
by Clare Connelly

A four-week paper marriage to Luca to save her family from destitution seems like an impossible ask for innocent Olivia... Until he says yes! And then, on their honeymoon, the most challenging thing becomes resisting her irresistible new husband...

### #3975 THE ITALIAN'S BARGAIN FOR HIS BRIDE
by Chantelle Shaw

By marrying heiress Paloma, self-made tycoon Daniele will help her protect her inheritance. In return, he'll gain the social standing he needs. Their vows are for show. The heat between them is definitely, maddeningly, *not*!

### #3976 THE RULES OF THEIR RED-HOT REUNION
by Joss Wood

When Aisha married Pasco, she naively followed her heart. Not anymore! Back in the South African billionaire's world—as his business partner—she'll rewrite the terms of their relationship. Only, their reunion takes a dangerously scorching turn...

**YOU CAN FIND MORE INFORMATION ON UPCOMING HARLEQUIN TITLES, FREE EXCERPTS AND MORE AT HARLEQUIN.COM.**

HPCNMRB1221

Van slid the door open and stepped inside only to have Becca
squeak and dance her feet, nearly dropping the groceries she'd
picked up.

"You knew I was here," he insisted. "That's why I woke you, so
you would know I was here and you wouldn't do that. I *live* here,"
he said for the millionth time, because she'd always been leaping
and screaming when he came around a corner.

"Did you? I never noticed," she grumbled, setting the bag on the
island and taking out the milk to put it in the fridge. "I was alone
here so often, I forgot I was married."

"*I* noticed that," he shot back with equal sarcasm.

They glared at each other. The civility they'd conjured in
those first minutes upstairs was completely abandoned—probably
because the sexual awareness they'd reawakened was still hissing
and weaving like a basket of cobras between them, threatening to
strike again.

Becca looked away first, thrusting the eggs into the fridge along
with the pair of rib eye steaks and the package of bacon.

She hated to be called cute and hated to be ogled, so Van tried
not to do either, but *come on*. She was curvy and sleepy and wearing
that cashmere like a second skin. She was shorter than average and
had always exercised in a very haphazard fashion, but nature had
gifted her with a delightfully feminine figure-eight symmetry. Her

ample breasts were high and firm over a narrow waist, then her hips flared into a gorgeous, equally firm and round ass. Her fine hair was a warm brown with sun-kissed tints, her mouth wide, and her dark brown eyes positively soulful.

When she smiled, she had a pair of dimples that he suddenly realized he hadn't seen in far too long.

"I don't have to be here right now," she said, slipping the coffee into the cupboard. "If you're going skiing tomorrow, I can come back while you're out."

"We're ringing in the New Year right here." He chucked his chin at the windows that climbed all the way to the peak of the vaulted ceiling. Beyond the glass, the frozen lake was impossible to see through the thick and steady flakes. A gray-blue dusk was closing in.

"You have four-wheel drive, don't you?" Her hair bobbled in its knot, starting to fall as she snapped her head around. She fixed her hair as she looked back at him, arms moving with the mysterious grace of a spider spinning her web. "How did you get here?"

"Weather reports don't apply to me," he replied with self-deprecation. "Gravity got me down the driveway and I won't get back up until I can start the quad and attach the plow blade." He scratched beneath his chin, noted her betrayed glare at the windows.

*Believe me, sweetheart. I'm not any happier than you are.*

He thought it, but immediately wondered if he was being completely honest with himself.

"How was the road?" She fetched her phone from her purse, distracting him as she sashayed back from where it hung under her coat. "I caught a rideshare to the top of the driveway and walked down. I can meet one at the top to get back to my hotel."

"Plows will be busy doing the main roads. And it's New Year's Eve," he reminded her.

"So what am I supposed to do? Stay here? All night? With *you*?"

"Happy New Year," he said with a mocking smile.

*Don't miss*
One Snowbound New Year's Night.
*Available January 2022 wherever*
*Harlequin Presents books and ebooks are sold.*

Harlequin.com

# IF YOU ENJOYED THIS BOOK
# WE THINK YOU WILL ALSO LOVE

## ⬧HARLEQUIN
# DESIRE

*Luxury, scandal, desire—welcome to
the lives of the American elite.*

Be transported to the worlds of oil barons, family dynasties,
moguls and celebrities. Get ready for juicy plot twists,
delicious sensuality and intriguing scandal.

**6 NEW BOOKS AVAILABLE EVERY MONTH!**

# *Love Harlequin romance?*

## DISCOVER.

Be the first to find out about promotions,
news and exclusive content!

**f** Facebook.com/HarlequinBooks

**𝕏** Twitter.com/HarlequinBooks

**⊙** Instagram.com/HarlequinBooks

**℗** Pinterest.com/HarlequinBooks

**You Tube** YouTube.com/HarlequinBooks

ReaderService.com

## EXPLORE.

Sign up for the Harlequin e-newsletter and
download a free book from any series at
**TryHarlequin.com**

## CONNECT.

Join our Harlequin community to
share your thoughts and connect
with other romance readers!
**Facebook.com/groups/HarlequinConnection**

# HARD AS NAILS
# Warriors

## TRACEY TURNER
### ILLUSTRATED BY JAMIE LENMAN

## Crabtree Publishing Company
www.crabtreebooks.com

# Crabtree Publishing Company
www.crabtreebooks.com
1-800-387-7650

616 Welland Ave.
St. Catharines, ON
L2M 5V6

PMB 59051, 350 Fifth Ave.
59th Floor,
New York, NY

Published by Crabtree Publishing Company in 2015.

**Author:** Tracey Turner

**Illustrator:** Jamie Lenman

**Project coordinator:** Kelly Spence

**Editors:** Becca Sjonger

**Proofreader:** Robin Johnson

**Prepress technician:** Samara Parent

**Print coordinator:** Margaret Amy Salter

Copyright © 2014 A & C Black

Text copyright © 2014 Tracey Turner

Illustrations copyright © 2014 Jamie Lenman

Additional illustrations © Shutterstock

First published 2014 by
A & C Black, an imprint of
Bloomsbury Publishing Plc.

Printed in Canada/022015/MA20150101

**Library and Archives Canada
Cataloguing in Publication**

Turner, Tracey, author
        Hard as nails warriors / Tracey Turner ;
illustrated by Jamie Lenman.

(Hard as nails in history)
Includes index.
ISBN 978-0-7787-1518-4 (bound).--
ISBN 978-0-7787-1517-7 (pbk.)

        1. Soldiers--Juvenile literature. 2. Military
history--Juvenile literature. I. Lenman, Jamie,
illustrator  II. Title.

U51.T87 2015        j355.0092'2        C2014-908092-1

**Library of Congress
Cataloging-in-Publication Data**

Turner, Tracey.
 Hard as nails warriors / Tracey Turner ;
Illustrated by Jamie Lenman.
    pages cm. -- (Hard as nails in history)
 Includes index.
 ISBN 978-0-7787-1518-4 (reinforced library
binding : alk. paper) --
ISBN 978-0-7787-1517-7 (pbk. : alk. paper)
1.  Military biography--Juvenile literature.  I.
Lenman, Jamie, illustrator. II. Title.

 U51.T85 2015
 355.0092'2--dc23

                                    2014046718